The Church
of
Little Bo Peep

and other stories

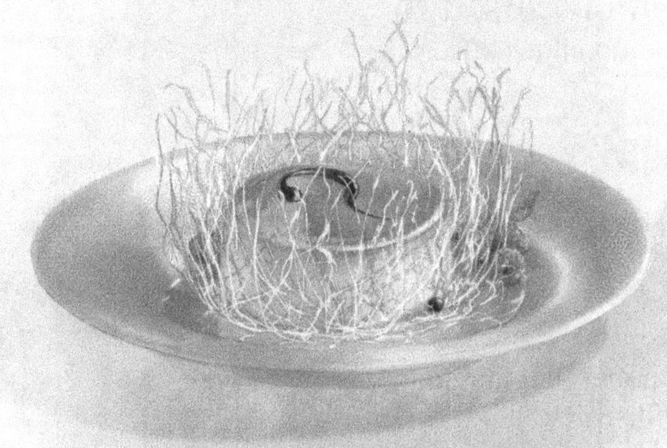

Jan Fancy Hull

Cover: Rebekah Wetmore
Editor: Andrew Wetmore
Author's photo: Betty Meredith

ISBN: 978-1-990187-10-0
First edition June, 2021

MOOSE HOUSE
PUBLICATIONS

397 Parker Mountain Road
Granville Ferry NS
B0S 1A0

moosehousepress.com
info@moosehousepress.com

We live and work in Mi'kma'ki, the ancestral and unceded territory of the Mi'kmaq People. This territory is covered by the "Treaties of Peace and Friendship" which Mi'kmaq and Wolastoqiyik (Maliseet) People first signed with the British Crown in 1725. The treaties did not deal with surrender of lands and resources but in fact recognized Mi'kmaq and Wolastoqiyik (Maliseet) title and established the rules for what was to be an ongoing relationship between nations. We are all Treaty people.

The characters in these stories grapple with questions. One discovers he had always posed them incorrectly; some hardly know what to ask; another realizes he had never dared question himself.

Do 'questions and answers' mean the same as 'lost and found'? If so, in what way? If not, why not?

Discuss.

And enjoy.

Jan Fancy Hull

This is a work of fiction. The author has created the characters, conversations, interactions, and events; and any
resemblance of any character to any real person, other
than as noted in the afterword, is coincidental.

The song quoted in *The Church of Little Bo Peep* is the traditional closing number of The Whiffenpoofs, an *a cap-
pella* group at Yale University. It was published in sheet
music form in 1909.
   The chorus, much of the style, and the scansion, though
certainly not the mood, derive from the Rudyard Kipling
poem "Gentlemen-Rankers".

For those who seek questions more than answers

Contents

Jan Fancy Hull

The Church of Little Bo Peep

Little Bo Peep

People may say about me—not that I care—that I'm not very sociable. I'm not anti-social. I believe in live and let live, just not live *with* so much. I don't join clubs or groups or crowds, but I don't mind if I'm invited to join in some *soiree* once in a while, or to attend a concert. Though riding on a bus would count as a group experience for me.

Not that I ride on buses.

I mention this because along with the usual bills and notices in my mailbox is a business envelope with a printed label addressed to me and a return label from *"See you, Seventy-two!"*

It's a dreaded university class reunion letter.

I did attend university, obviously, which had its moments, but that was thirty-five years ago. Whatever I learned there has long ago been put to use and/or paid for. I'm not in contact with my classmates from those days, nor do I have any lingering desire to see them. If I did, I would have.

I wasn't called to "See you" in 1982 or 1992 or '02, so this is of interest, slightly. Who has found me now, and why? I've not been hiding, but why am I found?

I'm reading the giddy announcement of the funtastic Class of '72 reunion when my phone rings. That's another thing that doesn't happen often but it's not rare enough to cause alarm.

"Hello?" I say.

"Hey, is that you, Laura?"

"Who's speaking, please?"

"Oh, sorry, hey, I thought you'd recognize my voice, even after all these years. Wanna guess?"

"No I do not. I'm hanging up now—"

"No-no-no, don't hang up, Laura, it's me, Jack! John 'Jack' Beaufort himself, live and in person!"

Damn. Why hadn't I let the call go to voice mail? "Jack. Well. *Quelle surprise*. How—to what do I owe this...?"

"Geez, Laura, don't sound so excited. Hey, how long has it been, twenty or more—"

"Judging by the mail I'm just opening, Jack, I'd have to say it is coming up on thirty-five years. To what do I owe this suspicious coincidence?"

"Oh great, you got the announcement. You're going, right?"

"To what?"

"To the reunion, natch. Well, specifically, to the great re-enactment."

"I haven't had time to read the exciting schedule of events yet, Jack, but I'm sure I'm busy that day, or evening, or weekend, or whenever it is. Too bad, I send my regrets, but I won't be able—"

"Aw, geez, Laura, just listen for a sec, willya? Do you have the program there now?"

"Unfortunately, yes."

"OK, good. Now just humour me and flip to the page where the Saturday schedule is. Got it?"

"Yes."

"Now, run your pointy finger down the page until you come to seven o'clock Saturday evening. What do you read there, Miss Laura?"

"I read 'The Great Re-Enactment: The Church of—' Jack, what the hell!"

"I know, isn't it great? Will you do it? You'll do it, right?"

"Do what? Will I make a fool of myself repeating a university spoof after thirty-five years of successfully forgetting about it *and* the people who made me do it?"

"Oh, come on, don't be like that. Listen, Laura, we—the committee—asked for it...for you, specifically. We—I worked hard to track you down."

"Your fingers must be very tired from all that walking. I've been in the book for decades."

"Yes but, I never knew, uh, what your name was. You know, somebody said you were, um..."

"Were what?"

"Well, um, married, sort of. You know. Partnered. Weren't you? Who knows what name women go by these days?"

"I know, Jack, it must be hard to find someone who insists on using her own full name and publishing it in the Halifax phone book year after year. How unfair of me. That must be why I've never received one of these invitations until now—just couldn't find me?"

"OK, Laura, will you please listen to me? The group is planning to get together next weekend to rehearse, and —"

"Jack, no. Thanks ever so, but no thanks. En-oh, no. I can't think of anything I'd rather not do more than that. Anyway, I no longer have the script, wouldn't know where to look for it."

"Ellen's got it."

"Who?"

"Ellen MacArthur. You know."

"Doctor Professor Ellen MacArthur? You've got her involved in this?"

"Yup. More than involved. She's in charge of these re-enactments for all the graduating classes. They've done one at most reunions. She kept all the files. Those projects were very popular, Laura, you remember that."

"I remember that I pretended to preach a very silly sermon about Little Bo Peep, and that our project got a C minus, if not a D. Not a good show for Honours students."

"Yes, but a standing ovation, too, remember that? Dr. MacArthur said she had to mark us down because you—I mean *we*—didn't satisfy some of the criteria for the project, but that's water long gone under the bridge. C'mon, Laura, what say? Will you at least come and see what's up? No obligation, okay? Starbucks, Saturday at three. I'll buy."

+++

Back in the day at my alma mater, I had a great English prof in my final year, my honours year, please and thank you, by name of Dr. Ellen MacArthur. She taught an elective writing class for fourth year English majors, one of which I was struggling to be. It was called Veristic Fiction 401. She said the 401 was not just for the class number but also for the famous highway in Ontario. She said that it was the busiest highway in North America, surprising but true (at least then).

Her whole first lecture in Veristic Fiction 401 was about Highway 401, until the closing sentence.

I forget how many people she said travelled on the 401 in the seventies but it's over half a million now, every day. She told us there was a section close to downtown Toronto called The Basket because the lanes weave over and under and around each other. I've never driven there and never will. That's what limos are for.

The 401 runs from Windsor to the Quebec border, so inevitably it goes through some countryside, but here's the kicker: the rural part was known as the Killer Highway because of the number of traffic accidents out there. The long, straight road bored the drivers, and inattention led to accidents. The grassy median wasn't wide enough to keep vehicles from bounding across it to smash into ones going the other way. Half a million traumatized people navigated The Basket more or less successfully every day; but out by the farms, mayhem.

She finished that first lecture with the admonition neither to kill our readers with boredom nor to make them weep with frustration at our complexities. If we could write scenic but challenging stories to carry them safely to our many destinations, she said, half a million readers might choose to travel our stories and come back for more.

I don't recall the subsequent lectures, likely because they were about writing fiction and, being unused for thirty-five years, are lost to me now. I remember that first lecture because it was so unexpected. *Quod erat demonstrandum*, I guess.

Dear Prof MacArthur. When did Jack start calling her Ellen? I don't recall that he was one of her favourites at the time. Maybe he ingratiated himself while working with her on class reunions. She must be retired by now.

Her class was known for the Veristic Fiction Practical assignment, and by 'known' I mean notorious. It's a wonder the Administration allowed it, because some years it was as riotous as the engineering students' infamous panty-raids. We didn't have engineers, though. We had a Divinity school, no less. In contrast to their alleged divinity, the creativity of some of Prof MacArthur's Veristic Fiction students was downright bawdy.

The point of the exercise was to create fiction as true-to-life as possible, hence the use of the *uber*-academic term "veristic". We weren't permitted to use the device of *deus ex machina*, meaning you couldn't rely on a miracle to rescue your story. We live in an age of miraculous discoveries, the Prof taught us, but nobody believes in miracles in the modern age; or, perhaps more accurately, miracles have no credibility. So when we write fiction, even science fiction, the twists and turns should be familiar, commonplace, making their miraculousness all the more believable. Edgar Allen Poe could terrify readers simply by inviting them down to the cellar to view a cask of Amontillado. Modern writers resort to death-ray guns and space monsters. But they only entertain, she said, they don't terrify in the same visceral way as Poe because readers don't see themselves in them. The readers don't expect to be in a spaceship, but they do have to go into their basements.

I guess I've remembered more of her lectures than I thought.

So, the assignment was to make a story. Not to write it, though we were required to submit our notes, but we had to make it happen in real time and as close to real life as legally possible, *ergo*, veristic. We didn't have to submit our proposals to the Prof in advance. She would simply grade us on the story as we presented it. A bit of theatre, I guess.

We had no ideas, and not having to show work in advance was a tar pit we rabbits ran toward.

By "we" I mean the aforementioned Jack, three or four other classmates who didn't get picked by the other groups, and me. One group created the 'Rendezvous of the Acadiens', a fictional reversal of the expulsion of the French from the province back in the mid-seventeen hundreds. The other group set up 'An Unlikely Romance' between one of the most notorious football players—his notoriety wasn't for football—and one of the female divinity students. They were not aware of the parts they were to play in the students' plot, not a good idea as it turned out.

My group had no idea what we were going to do. Jack had assured the Prof that we would do something big. We didn't have a clue what he had in mind. Then he arrived at the eleventh hour with his cockamamie plan and it was too late for us to avoid it.

+++

I don't tell Jack I'll go to Starbucks, nor do I say I won't. Who will be there, anyway, besides Jack? Who were those other classmates in our group? I can't dredge them up from my memory cells. To tell the truth, even when we were classmates I didn't know them outside of class. Would the Prof be there? It would be interesting to see her again, and I'd have to stay only for the duration of my coffee. I'll order an espresso, single shot, so I can be in and gone inside of ten minutes. I am a busy person, after all.

+++

"Hey, look everybody, it's Laura Lloyd!"

Everyone in the coffee shop looks, of course, so it's hard to tell how many are actually part of Jack's group. He's waving and grinning and attracting far too much attention. I quickly weave my way through the tables to where he is sitting with nobody I recognize.

The expressions on their faces indicate they don't recognize me either, or maybe they do but would rather not. The sentiment is mutual. Jack disappears as I sit down, so we all look at each other with the faces we have learned to wear in these situations.

"So," we all say in unison, and then wait for the others to speak. I surely do hate that.

"As everyone in the cafe has heard," I say, "I'm Laura. Forgive me if we've met before, but I think I'm sitting with strangers. Please tell me your names."

Ah, all my years on the higher rungs of the professional ladder do have residual benefits. Social graces rush in where angels fear to tread.

"Nice to see you again, Laura. It's me, Bob." He reaches across the table to shake my hand.

"Cyril." No handshake.

"Hi Laura. I'm Cy's wife, Elaine. I'm just here to—with Cy. Just ignore me."

"Hi, Laura. I'm not surprised that you don't remember me. I used to be—I mean—I'm Joann."

I never thought I'd be glad to see Jack under any circumstances, but he returns to the table at that moment and I'm relieved to yield the conversation to him. It's as if everyone there had been put away for countless years with their batteries still in them, and they have just enough juice remaining now to make short, ineffective gestures before their lights fade completely. Except for Jack, who has aged well. Meaning I do recognize him.

Am I like them? I can't be, please God. It takes a lot of energy to be who I am. And it takes a power plant to be sociable when you don't want to be.

"Here we go," Jack says, putting a ridiculous latte down in front of me, one of those excessively large bowls that belongs on the floor for a cat to drink from. So much for a quick single-shot; I'll be all afternoon working on that frothy pond.

"So," he continues, echoing our earlier *non sequitur*, but with far more enthusiasm. "I think that's the whole crew. Except for Ellen. She said she'd get here if she could, but she'd be late. Now—"

"Who's Ellen?"

"Gee, Bob, Ellen is none other than our revered English 401 Prof, remember? She has the files of all the productions of her Veristic Fiction class and can help us reproduce ours for the thirtieth reunion."

"What was her full name?" Bob asks the table top. "Ellen who?"

"Yes, Jack, I don't remember taking a class from any Ellen."

"That's because we knew her as Professor Doctor MacArthur back then, Joann," Jack says. "I've gotten to know her over the years since then, working on the reunions, and—well—we're grownups now, hey? And she's retired now, of course, so to me she's just Ellen— "

"Watch what you say about me, there, young Jack!" The voice is familiar and friendly. We all turn toward the speaker.

Thirty-five years have turned Cyril bald and fat. Joann, though I can't yet recall ever seeing her before, certainly looks like she is three and a half long and mediocre decades away from where we might have met. Bob looks ill. Jack looks great, but with too much exuberance for a man of his age. Our age. But this woman looks exactly like our professor and at the same time looks nothing like her. Youth isn't the only attractive age. Ellen MacArthur has definitely come of age, which is her late sixties, I'm guessing. Skin, hair, teeth, eyes, clothes, they all look brand-new on her, but her smile and presence make you understand that they are all genuinely hers.

"Now, don't tell me, let me guess," she says, taking the chair which Jack has convinced the people at a nearby table to give up, their coats now draped across their laps. "You're Bob, and that's Cy, nice to see you both again, and you must be Cy's better half. Welcome, I'm Ellen. Hello, Joann, I'd know you anywhere, and Laura, it's been too long. And hello again, Jack. Oh, Jack, just an espresso, single-shot, please. I can't stay long, I'm afraid."

My great first impression of Ellen—yes, you *do* get a second chance to make a first impression if it's thirty-five years later—is instantly alloyed with envy. Here's me thinking I have superior social graces and then Ellen swans in and greets us all by name, obviously having done her homework. *And* gets the beverage she wants, too, without any fuss. She has charmed us all, all over again.

Maybe I do spend too much time alone, outside of work. Maybe my social graces are only better than those of a houseplant. I have only my spider plant for comparison.

"Jack, bring me up to date on what you've discussed, if you don't mind. Sorry I was late, but—"

"Hey, no problem, Ellen. We were just getting reacquainted. We hadn't got to the details of the project yet. It's great that everybody is here from the original production, though, isn't it? We'll be able to do a complete reproduction. Some of the other groups had to leave out parts, like that romance group, remember them?"

"Never mind that," Ellen says briskly. "Let's stick to Veristic Fiction 401, spring of 1974, project title—um, let me see, I brought your file—ah, yes, here it is: 'The Church of Little Bo Peep'. Wonderful! Controversial, as I recall, but no harm done, none that would last into this century anyway. The established churches didn't fall, the sheep didn't take over the fold. My notes indicate that you didn't receive a very good mark for this project, though. Does anyone remember why, or want to confess anything?"

Ellen is sitting next to me. Under the scent of fresh air she brought in with her I can smell the musty old file she is holding, which does nothing to improve my memory.

The others are looking at our former Prof as though she is a bright television with the sound turned off—curious but not comprehending the show without the sound, and sure they can't afford it, anyway. What had they been told to convince them to come here? No more than I had been, evidently.

"Um, I think it was because our notes were incomplete," Jack ventures.

"Would you have had anything to do with that?" I ask Jack, not intending it to sound quite as sharp as it comes out.

"Oh, hey now," Jack replies.

"Laura, you always were so funny," Joann says. Her fawning is faintly familiar.

"What class was this, again?" This from Cyril. I search his face again for something to recognize.

"Fourth year honours English, Cy," Joann reminds him. "Veristic Fiction four-oh-one, remember? We had to act out a realistic fictional story. Our group did a—a church skit. You remember, don't you?"

"Yes, he remembers," Cyril's wife says. "He does. It takes him a while, that's all, but he does remember, don't you, dear?"

A cloud of discomfort passes over our little group, there in the midst of the Starbucks chatter and tootling music from the Andes, as we absorb that one of our contemporaries is losing, or has lost, his ability to remember things I have successfully forgotten. I bend low to take a few laps around my pool of milky latte. It tastes like a bowl of warm nothing.

"I didn't take any religion classes," Cyril says. Nobody pursues that.

"All right, let's get going on this," Jack says. For the first time, I am glad for his ebullience. Say what you have to say, Jack old boy, so I can get out of here.

"Ellen here has the old outline—what there is of it, sorry—and so, basically, all we have to do is reprise our parts on the Saturday night of the reunion weekend. We're the featured entertainment right after the dinner, so that'll be around eight o'clock, but we'll all be there for the dinner beforehand anyway, right?"

I am just about to draw breath to deliver my regrets, so sorry, when Ellen says, "I can work with you as a group for one rehearsal the Saturday prior, from three till four. Sorry I can't offer more, but I have a pretty tight schedule."

She pronounces it "shed-yule", not "sked-jewel" like everyone else I know, and that idiosyncrasy opens a window into my memory of her, of how hard she worked to help each of us do well. I'm sitting elbow to elbow with her now and I cannot at this moment think what I have done in thirty-five years to make use of what she tried to teach us in her classes—other than staying off Highway 401. Maybe I could re-inject some of her royal jelly into my life. I'm open to change, when it's for her kind of better. She's handed me an opening to do just that, on a one-hour platter.

"Would we have to memorize anything?" I ask, sounding like a grade school student. "I'm sorry, but we're all busy with work, I'm sure, and—"

"Oh, no-no-no," Jack says. "At these re-enactments everyone just reads their scripts. Of course, a little ad lib-bing is encouraged, right, Ellen?"

"That's right. This is for fun. The marks are ancient history and cannot be changed now—although I suppose in your case you might want to try." Ellen laughs.

"Who did what, Jack?" Joann asks. "I think I was dressed in some sort of costume, wasn't I?"

"You sure were, Joann. You were Little Bo Peep, re-member? Okay, here's the skinny: Joann was Little Bo Peep, in costume just as in the story book, with a crook and ringlets and all that. Bob and Cyril here were sheep, one white and one black, also in costume. I think we have your outfits reserved at a costume place in Dartmouth. Laura was the Preacher."

"Yes, well, definitely not type-casting," I say. "And you? What was your role, Jack?"

"I was the, um, usher. Shepherd, you could call it. I got the audience—the flock—into and out of the church. And I helped you write the script—the sermon."

"And there was a stink about it, wasn't there?" says El-len. "What set that off, now?"

"We put it on in the chapel?" Joann offers.

"Well, okay, I guess that would have offended some, but—"

"On Sunday morning," Jack says. "We went in just as chapel service was about to start. First I ushered in about a hundred students more than they had ever had at ser-vices, so the minister had to wait while we got everyone in, and then as he was about to start the service again, Laura here took over the pulpit and made him sit down, and these three came up to the front and wandered about a bit and then stood in a sort of tableau while Laura delivered her, um, sermon."

"Perhaps that was it," Ellen says, "the sacrilege and all that. I had to go mollify the big hats, not just Administration and Arts but Theology, too. Veristic Fiction class was nearly cancelled after that, but I gave it my best defence and prevailed. My, my, I wonder if they'd react the same way today. I should think they'd rejoice at all those students in chapel, no matter what drove them in."

"Yes, but," Jack says, "nobody stayed. Laura came down from the pulpit and Bo Peep and these two sheep went out. After I herded out all the extras, there were just the usual dozen divinity students left in the chapel. I think we made a point we didn't intend to make."

"What was the point, Jack?" asks Joann. "I often thought of that afterward. We didn't mean any disrespect. Did we? I know I didn't. I play the organ in my church."

I am tempted to tell her I've met some church organists who mean disrespect every Sunday, but I choose to keep quiet.

"The point was to make a good mark in your elective by bringing to life a fictional story in as realistic a way as possible," Ellen answers. "I personally was surprised that your classmates who enacted the Rendezvous of the Acadiens—potentially a very controversial issue—caused nary a ripple, even though they tried to force everyone on campus to speak French on the day or be expelled from the campus, you see, as the Acadians had been expelled from the province for not speaking English. A few of the profs actually tried to lecture in French that day. My own attempt was pathetic."

"And what happened with the living romance story?" I ask her. "There was some poop about that, too, wasn't there?"

"The less said about that, the better," is all Ellen will say.

"Yeah, okay," Jack says. "We've got lots to worry about right in front of us. Well, nothing to worry about, just some work to do, well, it's not work, we just—"

"Jack," I say, "what do you do for a living, may I ask?"

"Why?"

"Just curious. Catching up with you and all that. I'm in government, provincial civil service. You?"

"I'm with an ad agency. After university I sold advertising for local radio and TV stations, and then I went back to school to learn something practical—no offence, Prof—in marketing and PR. I've been at that ever since. I'm a partner now. Doing okay. "

"I'd say you're well-employed," I say, careful this time to sound positive, not snarky. "I think people would find it hard not to buy whatever you're selling. So, God help me, where and when do we rehearse?"

+++

I'm such a wimp. A social climber. A spineless kiss-ass. A lily-livered latte-licker.

Hey, watch that self-talk, there, Missy Laura. I lean over to frown at myself in the car's rear-view mirror to emphasize my point. *Be nice. Look on the bright side.*

And where would that bright side be, pray tell?

Well, the side where I get to be in the presence of someone who has some class, for a while. That's a positive. It never hurts to share space with greatness. All right, sometimes it does hurt. Sometimes the gap between me and people I admire is a shameful distance and I don't like to be reminded of it.

I want to be a good person, I really do. I even want to be nice once in a while, and smooth, and even—well—radiating, like Ellen MacArthur. I can do it sometimes. But people like her don't *do* it. They *are* it, whatever "it" is.

But I don't like everyone, as she appears to do. I didn't like anyone at our table this afternoon at the coffee shop, except Ellen. And then there's Jack. He doesn't seem to like or dislike anyone, he just ignores what anyone says and barrels on with his own plans. Good grief! Why did I agree to join this silly band of fools?

Maybe I am a little bit nice. As the Preacher in the stupid skit, my role was key, as I recall. None of the others could manage it now, that's for sure; certainly not Cyril, poor thing. If I don't do my part, they can't put on the skit and that would spoil their fun. It's big of me to do it.

To make sure the day isn't a total loss, I stop at the Jo Café on the way home, order myself a double-shot espresso and read what's left of the *Globe* on the table there.

+++

I'm surprised to see Cyril at the rehearsal, his wife hovering. I thought she would see the kindness in having him bow out of this charade, but apparently not. Our whole group is assembled in this little Chocolate Lake Hotel convention room where the moment of truth will take place next week.

Not only is Cyril here, he and Bob are standing at a piano. Joann is seated on the bench, and she is saying, as I enter the room, "That was very good, fellas. Gee! Now I remember why we got the standing ovation!"

Gee, my memory is that the standing ovation was for my part, but I'll let them have their moment. What they're singing sounds familiar:

We're poor little lambs who have lost our way,
Baa, baa, baa.
We're little black sheep who have gone astray,
Baa, baa, baa.
Gentleman songsters off on a spree,
Doomed from here to eternity.
Lord have mercy on such as we,
Baa, baa, baa.

They really ham it up, and I'm surprised at how well they sing.

Jack comes over to where I've seated myself and hands me Ellen's musty file. "Hey, Laura, about your script. As you'll see, it's a bit sketchy, so—"

"Isn't that *The Whiffenpoof Song*?"

"Oh, hey, yeah, remember? That was the, ah, the hymn they sang."

"Nervous as hell, as I recall," I say. "I guess there's no need to be nervous now. Our marks don't depend on my performance as they did back then."

"Right, right," Jack says. "You'll be great next week. Listen, Laura, I have to run to Dartmouth to get to the costume store before it closes. I think they've got everything we need. Can I ask, what, ah, what dress size you wear? These days?"

"What? Dress? I haven't worn a dress since pantsuits were invented. I don't want to wear a dress, Jack. What did you have in mind? Can't I wear my own clothes?"

"No no no, it's more of a...a gown. A robe. I think you wore a choir gown back then."

"Oh, that kind of dress. A costume. That's fine, then, I guess. Large should cover it. Tall, large, whatever. And modest, mind."

Jack starts toward the church hall door. I look around. Aside from the three performers at the piano, there's nobody else in the room. "Oh, Jack?" I call after him.

"'Sup?"

"Where's—was—is Ellen coming this afternoon?"

"Oh, she can't make it. She said to tell you to create a new speech as she must have lost the script out of the file. *Ciao*!"

Damn. I'd been hoodwinked into coming, mostly by myself. Whiffenpoof, indeed.

I open the file and review the scant notes therein. They consist of the words to the song being rehearsed, and a sheet of paper on which is written, perhaps in Ellen's handwriting, "Make it up yourself this time".

What the hell.

When the singers have declared themselves sung out, I take the file up to the piano and ask them to help me piece the program together.

+++

"Why are there no notes? What am I supposed to...I mean, is it supposed to be funny?"

I'm on the phone with Jack, who is trying to convince me that I can extemporize on the absent text of thirty-five years ago.

"Well, yes and no," he says, not helpful at all. "Just do it straight and I think that'll be funny. That's what you did, I'm pretty sure. The more serious you are, the more they'll enjoy it. What's that called?"

"Farce, I think," I say. "Didn't we major in English? We should know. This'll be a farce, anyway."

"Well, that's not a bad thing, is it? I mean, when you intend to be farcical, you're not the fool, it's what you're aiming at that is the butt of the joke, right? We use this approach lots in marketing. Especially politics."

It annoys me when annoying people make good points.

+++

The details of our childish skit aren't worth repeating, except for my part, as it has a bearing on the rest of my story, odd as that may appear.

Jack is a red-vested wolf in sheep's clothing, not a passive shepherd. After a theatrical throat-clearing he proclaims the faux scripture, the child's poem "Little Bo Peep". I'm in the costume Jack supplied, but this is no drab choir gown. This shimmering thing has wings and a halo and I'm wearing the glitter makeup I was given. It's like the Angel Gabriel has crash-landed on the Tooth Fairy. In short, I'm spectacular.

The audience applauds my entrance. I stand as regal as the Sun Queen and deliver my sermon—from memory—in a voice like that of *The Wizard of Oz*'s Glinda, the Good Witch:

The Church of Little Bo Peep – Meditation on The Great Rhyme
[Old Idea]
1. Little Bo Peep
2. has lost her sheep,
3. and doesn't know where / to find them.
[New Idea]

1. Leave them alone
2. and they will come home,
3. wagging their tails / behind them.

Dearly Beloveds, our topic today is "Be Ye Neither Lost Nor Found", based on Old Idea, phrase 2: "...has lost her sheep..." and New Idea, phrase 1: "...leave them alone..." Many may question *The Great Rhyme*, but wisdom is found in meditating upon it.

In New Idea, Phrase 1, "Leave them alone", you are not told to *be* alone. This is not said *to* you at all, but *about* you. It is spoken over your head, as it were, a command to all who would dictate how you should live. "Leave them alone." It couldn't be more clear.

Beloveds, this New Idea teaching is so needed in our time. The Old Idea implies that we were possessions of someone, or somewhere, or something, and that we should meekly obey that person, place or thing. Old Idea believers seek to justify this concept with their dogma.

The New Idea flatly orders them to "Stop it!"

[Here I wield my wand in the air like a broadsword.]

We are reminded, in reading this passage, that we must be very careful of whom we choose to govern us when governing is required, as it sometimes may be.

But what did the Old Idea mean by "lost"? The dictionary says it can mean: "gone out of one's possession." Veristically, you are no one's possession, beloveds. You are too precious for that. Possession is for things.

Hear me, now: *if you cannot be owned, you cannot be lost.* Oh, you do sometimes feel lost, don't you, when you have strayed from your path, but only you can know when you are on it again.

Hear me, now: *if you cannot be lost, you cannot be found.* If someone claims to have found that which is not lost, is he not a liar, or a thief? Therefore, do not possess each other, beloveds, neither be anyone's possession. Be kind to your good selves.

"Leave them alone!" How sweet the sound! Amen and Amen!

Next week's meditation will be: "Bo Peep: loser or leader? Can everyone change?"

The audience greeted this with thunderous applause, to my great surprise. Then there was a sanctimonious vocal performance of another nursery rhyme by Bob, Cyril and Joann, while other conscripted sheep passed buckets amongst the crowd, who tossed folding money into them.

Baa Baa Black Sheep, have you any wool?
Yes, sir, yes, sir, three bags full.
One for my master, and one for my dame,
One for the little boy who lives down the lane.
Baa Baa Black Sheep, have you any wool?
Yes, sir, yes, sir, three bags full.

I stay for the after-party. It doesn't seem right for me to bolt right after our standing ovation. We're all still in costume. For me, that's key. Mine's impressive, and I don't mind wearing impressive at times like this. I wouldn't be able to tolerate that crowd without a costume.

The "three bags full" the sheep gathered from the audience made a significant subsidy of the cash bar, so everyone is buying discounted drinks for everyone else. Consequently, I drink too much, just to go along. The plonk-in-a-box on offer tastes better by the third glass.

I'm greeted by so many people asking "Remember me?" that I wonder if I had gone on to grad school. I couldn't have had that many classmates in just four years, could I?

"Oh, hi there, my goodness, look at you!" I say.

We're all bullshitting. We're all drunk. So when I finally change out of my costume and look for my keys to drive home, I'm glad I can't find them, though they must be in my bag. I have my credit card tucked in my bra—a trick learned long ago—so I take a room in the hotel and crash.

+++

In spite of several noisy after-after parties going on in other rooms nearby, I sleep like a wine-soaked log. If I were in water I wouldn't float. What do they call those? Deadheads. That's what I feel like, except my head is rather too much alive for me.

There's a tapping at my door. "Housekeeping."

Hell. What time is it?

"What time—?" I can't ask that, partly because it sounds stupid and partly because my head doesn't like me to speak loudly at the moment.

I drag a sheet off the bed to wrap myself in and stumble to the door so I can speak more quietly. "What time is...checkout?" I wheeze through the closed door.

"Eleven o'clock, ma'am."

"Well, come back after eleven, then," I say, annoyed.

"It is after eleven, ma'am," Housekeeping says plaintively. "It's almost noon."

Hell and damn. I've overslept for work, my car's in a tow-away zone, my cat will be going wild. Settle down. Think. What day is it? Um. Um. Weekend-day. Oh, phew. Not a work day, at least.

"Be right out," I say to Housekeeping. "Sorry."

I have no idea if Housekeeping is still there or if she has gone on to pretend to clean another room with her carpet rake and room-freshener aerosol spray.

I call room service to order coffee and dry toast but they will send only coffee. They don't serve toast after twelve, imagine that. I mean, no wonder businesses are hurting. When the coffee comes it's undrinkable.

In the shower I wonder why, when I wake suddenly, do I think I have a cat at home shredding my tapestries. I have neither.

The bill is already under my door so I bypass the checkout process, hoping they won't bill my card for overtime. I find my keys in my bag, and make a speedy exit from the parking lot, hoping not to run into any of my co-celebrants from last night. My luck holds.

I'm through the roundabout before I notice a scrap of paper tucked under my windshield wiper. Whatever they're selling, I don't want it. I flick on the wiper to get rid of it but it won't go. It appears to be taped to the blade. A prankster must have put it there, one of my new best friends from last night, perhaps.

When I get home, I am relieved to see that everything is where I left it only yesterday. My spider plant is fine. I remind myself of what tomorrow's work will entail, get something out to wear for it and very soon I'm back in bed, to sleep this time, rather than pass out.

I'm very glad I live alone at a time like this. I couldn't abide a look of disapproval from anyone who is not my bathroom mirror, nor do I want to hear anyone ask if I've learned anything from this. Of course I have. I learned it all a long time ago, many times over. And I'll likely learn it again.

+++

The smudged note on my windshield is from Jack.

> LAURA – BRAVO!
> ELLEN SAYS WE EARNED AN A+
> **PLEASE <u>PLEASE</u> CALL ME 555-4321 ASAP.**
> JACK

I assume the 'please call' is about returning the gown. The costume shop label is inside the gown, so at noon on Monday I run it across the bridge to Dartmouth myself.

The rest of the week I'm on the move, out of town twice. Perhaps I didn't mention, but I have an important job in the provincial Civil Service. I'm the Director of Decision Support. I won't explain what that is; you can look it up. Not all government functions are stars like Health or Highways, thank goodness. Somebody has to keep the wheels turning in the provincial government while all the pretty boys and girls are out front grandstanding. I fell into my niche back in the early eighties when it was in early development stages, and I rode the wave to where I am today. And where I am today is poised to apply for Deputy Minister of the department in about a year when the current Deputy retires. Or I'll retire.

My Honours English degree did not figure in this career in any way, except to equip me to write very readable analyses of the data for those who make, or at least announce, the big decisions. Politicians and senior civil servants think in words—or pictures or maybe stick drawings—not binary code, and they appreciate how I interpret data for them. I'm very good at my job. I'd be successful in any career I chose, maybe even better at something I really enjoyed doing.

My pension credits are pretty much at maximum now, so working for future earnings will soon be redundant. It's crazy, but that's the civil service train I got on and that's where it takes all who manage to stay aboard.

Has lost her sheep

One year later

Normally, I don't check my home voice mail until the weekend. I don't get many unexpected personal calls, and I wasn't expecting any this particular week. That's not as bad as it sounds. People know I frequently work five twelve-hour days, plus much of many Saturdays. There's always the mail. I work in the electronic world, but I don't live in it.

When I check my phone this weekend, there are four messages from Jack Beaufort, first asking nicely, then reminding, repeating, and finally begging for us to get together, "just for a quick chat". To put an end to these messages, I call back when I'm sure to get his voice mail, and give him a time on Sunday, and a café. I make sure I arrive ten minutes early and order my own coffee.

"Hey, Laura, great to see you. Wow!"

Wow people annoy me. They fill the air with empty vowel sounds, like dogs barking.

"Hello, Jack. How are you?"

Jack wants to review last year's reunion. I let him roll while I scan the documents I had brought to work on. I'm not a workaholic, but I do feel I need to work nearly all the time. Not just to keep up, but to keep ahead, which is my minimum standard.

"So then I got to thinking, Laura," he's saying.

"Hmm?"

"Well, I mean, you really have a knack for it. I mean, more than a knack. You missed your calling, if you ask me."

"Excuse me, Jack, I missed what? My calling?" I put down my pen and look up at him. "What are you talking about now?"

"Leading, er, public speaking, um, preaching. You're a natural at it. Geez, Laura, you had everyone right in your hands. That's what I wanted to tell you, after the reunion. I know we all got a bit goobered, but don't you remember what people were saying?"

"No, can't say I do."

"Well, I do, and some of 'em wrote letters, too. The re-enactment was entertaining, no doubt about that, but the audience was interested, Laura, and *moved*."

"By what, again?"

"By *you*, Laura. By what you said. How you got all that meaning out of a nursery rhyme is beyond me. They would've stayed for more, I'm sure. Well, except for the subsidized bar."

This is why I've avoided these people for all those years. "They were moved by a woman in a drag queen gown who rambled on about a fairy-tale rhyme in mock-preacher style?"

"Well, okay, the gown, but." Jack is tenacious. "It was what you said, not how you were dressed. Don't you re-member, about how Bo Peep—" he lowers his voice and leans forward in case the lovers and caffeine addicts in the café might overhear "—how Bo Peep was wrong to think she owned us? You said we can't be owned, that anyone who says they own us is a liar, that we're free to be ourselves. I haven't forgotten it, obviously. It's like total absolution or freedom or something. It really reson-ated, Laura."

"Jack," I say, "I made up what I hoped was an amusing little sermonette, which 'Little Bo Peep' lent itself to, as I recall. I had to start from scratch, thanks to Ellen MacArthur's empty file, *and* on short notice, *and* in the midst of a very busy time at work, as all times are. And by the way, since you have opened that little door in my memory for me, why do you suppose there were no notes at all in our file? What was so bad about the original that Prof MacArthur—Ellen to you—gave us such a bad mark and then expunged it from the record?"

Jack looks left and right in that *film noir* clichéd mannerism that accompanies a confession or confidence. "You really don't know?"

"Not if I'm asking, Jack."

"Does the name Johnny Standley mean anything to you?"

"Was he in our class, too?"

"What? No. Do you recall hearing the phrase, 'It's in the book'?"

"Other than as it pertains to phone numbers, no."

"Okay. I've never told this to anyone," Jack says, drawing a deep breath. "Laura, in 1952, Johnny Standley, a comedian, did a monologue as a preacher. He used Little Bo Peep as his, um, sermon. It was released as a single and went to number one on the pop charts, which says something about comedy and pop charts in those days. It was called 'It's in the Book'."

"In nineteen fifty-two?"

"Nineteen fifty-two."

"Are we about the same age?" I ask.

"You and me? I—I guess so. I was born in 1951."

"Close enough. Therefore, we were in cloth diapers when this phenomenal entertainment event shook the world. My memory does not pre-date potty training. What's your point, Jack?"

"I'm getting to it, Laura, give a guy a chance. 'It's in the Book' sold a million copies, believe it or not, one million copies. Were there even a million record players on the planet then? I suppose there was little else for entertainment, not like now. Anyway, here's the thing: my father had one of those records, and he played it all the time when I was a kid. When we got that Veristic Fiction assignment, and nobody could think of what to do in it—"

"Hold it right there, buster," I say. "I don't recall much about it, but I do remember that you wouldn't meet with the rest of us to help plan what we were going to do. Own up, now."

"Well, okay, that's true, Laura, sort of. But the reason I couldn't meet with you and Cy and the others, is because I went home to my parents' place that weekend and dug out the old vinyl record. I played it over and over to get the script copied out, more or less, and that's what I gave you to read for our assignment. I'm sorry, Laura. Are you mad at me?"

"You plagiarized our fiction assignment?"

"Uh, yes."

"Amazing. Well done, Brutus. But how did MacArthur find out what you did?"

"She's about ten years older than we were—are. A million copies were sold. You do the math."

"I hate that expression."

"Sorry. I mean she most likely heard it on the radio. Maybe had a copy in her own home, though it doesn't seem like her kind of funny, now that I think of it."

"Was my performance of it anything like Top of the Charts, Jack?"

"Ah, no, sorry, not at all. You read it too seriously, like you were in church reading from the Bible, and it, well, it wasn't a big hit, shall we say."

"Really. So, mystery of the low mark solved. Why didn't she fail us entirely, then? Or have us expelled? Or you, at least?"

I'm more amused than annoyed at Jack's confession, I have to say. I had been duped, carried out the ruse in ignorance, but they granted my degree anyway, *cum laude*. No skin off my nose, not that I like that expression, either.

"Well, I don't know if you want to go there," Jack says.

"The hell I don't. Don't stop now, penitent-boy. Let's hear it all. It'll do you good to confess."

"I'm not so sure." He exhales and looks at me with such a guilty expression that I want to laugh. "When Ellen called me in, as our group leader, to inquire about the script—your script—I told her...that you had brought it to the group—"

"You what?"

"Hang on. Yes, I told her that we thought you wrote it. You were her favourite and I figured she'd give you more, um, leeway. I argued on your behalf—please wait, Laura —that because it sold a million copies it would have been in the air all around us in our formative years, so you wouldn't have known where you might have acquired the preacher-act idea. A bad imitation of Standley's act wouldn't be plagiarism any more than using the nursery rhyme would be. I said it was in the public domain, sort of."

"That wouldn't be correct."

"I know, but the Prof wasn't eager to take you down, as I expected, or to get involved in a public argument over it. In the end, she decided to settle for a low mark for our project because she said, uh, she said you had given it such a bad performance that it sort of compensated for the plagiarism. There. Geez, it's finally out. Whew!"

Imagine being relieved to confess that you had defended innocence with a lie.

You know those dreams where you're at a murder scene, and then you realize with horror that the bloody knife or smoking gun is in your own hand? I have one periodically. Well, I feel that kind of horror at this moment. I am also feeling a growing urge to make the dream come true.

"Look," I say, putting my papers in my portfolio and reaching for my jacket, "this is all water under the bridge. Though I didn't realize when I met Ellen MacArthur last year that she thought she was seeing a plagiarist when she looked at me, thanks to your lie. I'm sorry about that, but nothing to be done about it now. Unless...are you—do you see Ellen these days, Jack? You might want to 'fess your little indiscretion to her, sorta take the egg off my face, hey, Jacko?"

I don't want it to, but I find this little story is really getting under my skin. I work hard to keep my nose clean. This is the sort of dirt that a background investigation of a prospective Deputy Minister might uncover. I did nothing wrong, but nobody's innocent in the press these days.

"Oh, Laura, I'm so sorry. But please don't go yet. I really do have something I want to discuss with you, about—"

"I'm not interested, Jack Be Nimble. Little Bo Peep's been done. She's lost this sheep and I don't give a damn. Leave it alone, remember? Cheerio."

+++

Jack doesn't give up easily. He calls several times and I delete his messages without listening to them. I hear enough pleadings and excuses in my work day to do me. People think if they explain why they screwed you, you will see them as victims of circumstance rather than the quislings they are, and you will be somehow un-screwed. I am not so easily duped. I subscribe to the maxim: fool me once, shame on you; fool me twice, shame on me.

Even so, my spidey-senses don't tingle when I receive a message from Ellen MacArthur some months later, inviting me to join her for a drink after work at the wine bar in the hotel at the Willow Tree corner. As that is my regular stop on my way home from work, it's easy enough to acquiesce. I leave her a message advising that seven o'clock is my earliest definition of 'after work'.

It's closer to seven-thirty when I arrive at the bar. Huston has already made my first drink, stirred just the way I like it, if somewhat melted now. I take it off my tray behind the bar and join Ellen at her table by the wide windows overlooking the busy intersection, the broad Common, and my condo beyond.

"Laura! So good to see you again. Thank you for agreeing to meet me."

Ellen looks fresh and fabulous, and that little mouse of envy gnaws at my ego again. I was fresh twelve hours ago. I am never her kind of fabulous.

"Pardon my tardiness, but the Minister decided she needed something complicated this very afternoon. Legislature is in session, as you are no doubt aware."

"Of course. Do you work under the principle that you can do the difficult right away, but the impossible may take a little longer?" Ellen's eyes twinkle.

"Something like that, yes," I say, "although it all seems to take longer than people are willing to allow. These days all we are asked for is the impossible."

A sip of my melting martini is medicine. Ellen has a glass of white wine in front of her, lipstick on the rim but little gone from the contents. Not a drinker, perhaps.

"Laura," Ellen begins, "Jack Beaufort told me—"

"Really, Ellen." I hold up my hand. "I have no interest in reviewing Little Bo Peep or Jack Beaufort's indiscretions. Please don't concern yourself with that."

"Hear me out, Laura," Ellen counters, holding up her own elegant hand. "Jack confessed about making you the 'fall guy' for that English project. It is understandable that you would be chagrined, or worse, even now, believing I thought you dishonest. I'm glad he set the record straight, though in the grand scheme of the past three decades, it is a very small thing, to my way of thinking."

"Well, thanks for that. I agree, my life and career have been unimpeded by Jack's university prank, if you can call lying and framing someone else for academic dishonesty a prank. I must confess, with respect, Professor, that I hadn't given your class much thought after graduation until I got entangled in that reunion fiasco. The bonus of all that was seeing you again, so my embarrassment due to Jack's recent confession was more acute than it deserved to be. Let's forget that now, shall we? Please tell me, to what do I owe the pleasure of your invitation to meet here? Oh good—food. Please help yourself, Ellen. Thank you, Huston."

Huston, the head waiter at the wine bar, has quietly placed napkins on our laps and now serves something he and the chef have decided I would like, which today is an array of hot and cold tapas.

"Thank-you, Laura. Did you order this? It looks delicious but I don't recall—"

"Standing order. They know me here."

"Excellent. Well, to answer your question, there are two reasons. I enjoyed seeing you again at the reunion last year, and since we've both learned the truth of all those years ago, I wanted you to know I knew that, too. The other reason, however, still has to do with your nemesis, the inimitable Jack Beaufort."

I never swear at work, or aloud anywhere if I can help it. There are a lot of things I don't do at work that I would like to do, but you don't get ahead by giving in to your petty urges, certainly not in the civil service. I feel like swearing now at the repetition of Jack's name, but I don't, in deference to Ellen MacArthur, who doesn't seem to be the swearing kind. So I raise my eyebrows and tilt my head to indicate that she may continue.

"Jack, as you know, has an agency that does PR and advertising and all that. He is in charge of a *pro bono* fundraising project for United Way. His task is to organize a dinner theatre or some such thing at the World Trade Centre, and he wants the theme to be—"

Ellen hesitates and looks at me. My eyebrows are still up, so she continues.

"To be the 'Church of Little Bo Peep.' Not the 1950s original—what was it?—'According to the Book' or something like that? He wants it as you did it in your class reunion. Your modern version."

"'It's in the Book,'" I say. "Have you ever seen it? You should look it up online, Ellen. I did. No wonder you gave me a low mark. Had I seen or even known about the original version I would've played it up more, or tried to, at least. I completely misunderstood it based on what little information Jack gave me. I thought I was supposed to be serious. When I wrote that *ersatz* sermon for the reunion, I chose farce as the best approach. I certainly couldn't treat a nursery rhyme seriously now. I've matured, perhaps. One can hope."

A fresh glass quietly replaced my empty one, this one fresh, cold, crisp, the ice cubes tinkling my favourite tune.

"Anyway, Ellen, I'm a senior civil servant, not a dinner-theatre actor. Please tell Jack to find someone who will do his project justice."

"It's a celebrity project," Ellen says. "No actors. Prominent citizens and all that."

"All the more reason to look elsewhere. I'm not a prominent citizen, though I serve many of the usual suspects."

"You think not? Your name's been in the papers recently. That's prominence in Halifax."

The imminent retirement of my current Deputy Minister had become something of a *cause célèbre*, not because anyone understands or cares about our work, but because some in Opposition had got it in their heads that there might be nepotism afoot to fill the vacancy. This may be good for my chances, as I'm not related to anyone on the green side of the sod. I'm not implicated in the scandal-in-the-making, of course, but I'm frequently mentioned as a possible alternative. The consultants responsible for hiring have begun to hunt through my closets, as unobtrusively as they can, to see if any skeletons could be hanging in them. I think the job is mine to lose.

"It's a delicate prominence, then, Ellen. It's not of my making, and it could go all pear-shaped in a nano-second, and that's called notoriety, not prominence. Dressing me up as a fairy godmother who mocks organized religion at a time like this could be counterproductive, with all due respect to the needy served by the United Way. How about I make a nice donation instead? Everyone believes senior civil servants are grossly overpaid, so I could give as though that were true, if you like."

"You're very cynical, Laura," Ellen says, "but I suppose you've earned the right. I had enough of bureaucracy in the halls of academe, and we were far more cloistered from public scrutiny than you in government. Anyway, I respect your wish for obscurity, but I ask you to give this event serious consideration. If your name is being bandied about, but there's no actual Laura around to put a face to it, then you leave your character to others to flesh out—and they may not care how they do it in the end."

Thud. That's the sound of a solid argument landing at my feet.

I do what I've always done when I need a moment to consider what to do next: I change the subject. "Tell me, Ellen, I know you're retired from teaching, but what do you do to occupy your fine mind in retirement? Oh, sure, Huston, maybe I will tonight. Just a wee one. Ellen?"

Ellen asks for coffee. I usually stop at two drinks at the bar during the week, but all this talking has made me thirsty.

"My fine mind is home quite a lot," Ellen laughs. "I'm caregiver for my husband, and he often needs my attention suddenly and for unpredictable lengths of time. Between times he's as good as he ever was, so I'm able to get out...but never for long, and I can't really commit to anything regular."

"Good God, Ellen, that sounds like hell. May I ask what is your husband's affliction?"

"It is hell, thanks, especially for Henry. He had a great mind in his day, and still does by times, though one is less willing to rely on it now as it has let us down so many times in recent years. He has a mysterious disease that looks like dementia when he's in its grasp, but it withdraws for indeterminate periods, which dementia doesn't. It's rare enough that it hasn't been given a non-medical name for consumers."

"Care-givers? Nursing home? Any help?"

"Not yet. When he's in the grip of whatever it is, he can't tolerate anyone around but me, and neither of us can face the thought of him in a nursing home, at least not yet. Perhaps later, when his periods of, oh, delusion are more continuous. His motor skills will diminish, too."

"I'm very sorry to hear of all that, Ellen. You both should be enjoying the fruits of your labours in these golden years, instead of dealing with a nameless monster."

"Thank you. We do to the extent that we can. We read together, we follow sports and nature shows on the television, PBS programs, that sort of thing. Henry is researching a book—he was a political scientist, perhaps you didn't know, pretty well-respected in his field in his day. He's working on a modern model for democracy, an alternative to what he calls the failed version we have which gives the masses one tiny opportunity to vote once every four years or so, and gives too much power to the parties, not to the popular vote."

"He's got a point there, all right," I say. "And he has a better idea?"

"Yes, he does. Fortunately, a former colleague is working on it with him. I fear when it is published it will be just another book, good for some chatter but not likely to change things."

"Or it might start a revolution. That could be a good thing."

"Not for you, I think," Ellen says. "The civil service, at all levels, is in his sights. Beware!" She follows this with a warm smile.

"I'll consider myself forewarned, and please accept my gratitude for the heads-up," I say, a little more warmly than usual, but three drinks on a Wednesday evening do make one feel warm.

We both look at our watches and say "Time to go" in unison. "You'll be having a very late supper tonight, I'm afraid," Ellen says.

"This was my supper," I reply, gesturing to the half-cleared plate of tapas. "Not even the cat would eat my cooking during the week. So listen, when is this thing that Jack is doing, do you know?"

"Late spring, I think," Ellen says. "May I tell him you'll consider it?"

Do I need yet another reason to watch my intake of alcohol when in the company of charming humans? First I start to like them, then I get drawn into liking what they like. I mistrust emotion. Business is safer territory. I am stone-cold sober whenever there is a whiff of work around, no worries about that. Decision Support is my stage and I know how to play on it better than anyone. I can dish out supporting data faster than you can bake a cherry pie, Billy-boy. Quicker'n a cat can wink an eye.

Huston signals the doorman to hail me a cab.

And doesn't know where to find them

I didn't get the job.

In what the military would call a complete snafu, the court of public opinion swung the so-called arm's-length decision in favour of the Minister's nephew. Someone successfully argued that the rule against nepotism was against family values. I couldn't make that up. Rules should rule. When popular memes rule, beware.

Here's a little lesson, a snippet from my years of experience: start with any premise, fact or fake, and you can reach any conclusion you want. Inferring a conclusion from two known premises is called *syllogism* in logic, upon which the field of Decision Support is based, or ought to be. However, there is a trap in this branch of logic for amateurs who presume to dabble. For instance, if one argues that a small handful of pebbles doesn't make a pile, and that adding one more pebble will not either, then you *could* conclude that no additional number of pebbles will make a pile. That is a corrupted syllogism, or a *sorites* paradox. Most civilians don't care about that, but I had to, every day. I can't tell you the number of times I was asked to find proof that no number of additional pebbles would make a pile, or that removing an inde-terminate number of pebbles would turn a pile into a co-incident, unrelated set of pebbles.

Anyway, the Minister's nephew is said to be of average intelligence (a specious claim, though he has some qualifications) and has a family of his own, and since family values rank above all other attributes, especially during election campaigns, the nephew is therefore determined to be the best and smartest person for the deputy position.

I, in contrast, am of above-average intelligence (demonstrable and verifiable), know the department inside out, and get along passably with Ministers of all stripes, including this man's aunt, who will not be re-elected anyway. I'm not a member of her family, thus I rate behind her dog, which is undoubtedly very smart. I don't have dependants, so I don't "need" the job. I can't reveal who said that to me, because if he is found dead, which would not be a bad thing, I will be an unrepentant murder suspect.

Corrupted syllogisms abound.

But I'm not bitter.

As I may have mentioned, I've been jogging on that career treadmill for many years, and the quest for the Deputy position kept me in the game long after Decision Support lost its sexy appeal. As mentioned, my pension just about equals my comfortable salary, which is far beyond my simple needs, especially since I 'don't have family'. Spare me.

I've been asked to remain as Director, reporting to Boy Wonder. Who needs that?

I've read about retirement and all the boo-hooing that goes on when new retirees find themselves lost without a job to provide structure to their days. Hooey. I have a stack of pretty travel brochures and I'm looking forward to working my way through them, and when I've gone to all those places I'll order more. Northern hemisphere,

Down Under, Far East, Out West. I'll try scrabbling up some sacred character-building mountain, or being carried in a litter across a burning desert by handsome and deferential men who will lower me onto a perfumed rug and serve me dates and— well, no reason to delay bringing those visions into reality. Better to do it while I still bear some resemblance to the plum of my youth rather than the prune of my approaching old age.

So I retire.

I'm not stupid. Over several days, I quietly clean out my desk, take home documents I prefer to dispose of in private, wipe my computer's hard drive, and then present my resignation, effective immediately. I'm not going to walk out with that degrading cardboard box of bobble-headed desk detritus, as so many of my employees and colleagues have done over the years. My desk surface was always mirror-clear anyway.

There is a hastily-arranged Farewell & Welcome party for me and wonder-boy at the Five Fishermen restaurant. I hope everyone has a good time. I don't go.

+++

In the course of working on the United Way fundraising event with Jack Beaufort and occasionally Ellen MacArthur, I thaw a bit with Jack, especially as he learns how to deal with me: be straight and don't crowd me. He's still pushy, but that's his nature; and it's a strategy, too. In the latter half of my career, my employees were obliged to *obey* me. Jack's career is about *persuading* people to do what his clients want them to do, such as buy their cars or vote for their party or fly their airline. I find this interesting to observe, so I don't mind it so much when I catch him applying it to me. And I'm trying not to be annoyed when he doesn't obey me.

The *Little Bo Peep Gala* at the World Trade Centre is a smashing success. Not that I can take any credit for that. When such events are announced, individuals of means and corporations purchase tickets as a matter of course. The entertainment is secondary to the cause, as it should be.

But it doesn't hurt if people enjoy themselves, which they do. As Ellen said, it was a celebrity thing, so I'm rubbing elbows with Halifax's "names", including the Mayor, Archbishops of all leanings, the developer of a controversial project (as they all are in this town), and a few of the city's many university presidents. Believe me, putting those men and women in black and white sheep's costumes shouldn't be reserved for special occasions; it should be done every day. They ham it up and have the crowd in stitches. All I have to do is play it straight in another garish gown, which I find oddly empowering. It's camouflage, anyway. I give it my best.

The Deputy controversy is still being chattered about and I don't want to do anything that would lead people to think the right decision had been made after all, so I'm on my best behaviour, meaning I'm soberer than the several judges who are there, who are not.

+++

I'm not in any hurry to pack my bags for overseas travel. I want to explore my own beautiful province first. I haven't gone for a Sunday drive for ages. I have a fine car, expensive and comfortable, and I've dreamed about taking its computerized suspension around the bumpy country roads to see the leaves turn colour in the autumn light.

See? Decades in provincial civil service haven't drained me of all my humanity. I think I have a lot of humanity. I just never considered it relevant in the workplace.

I've just returned from one of those day trips, complete with a basket of rosy, fragrant, just-picked apples. I'm peeling off my driving gloves when the phone rings, still a strange sound in my apartment. I pick up the phone without checking to see who it is first. I'm getting slack.

"Yo, Laura, it's me." Jack, of course. "Want to have supper with me?"

No, not really.

"Sure," I say. "You called just in time. I just got back from the Valley and find I have nothing for supper but apples. I'll bring you one."

Jack wants to meet at the Inn on the River, beyond the edge of the city, out towards the airport. Food is good out there, but I suggest an Italian place in Bedford, it being somewhat closer. He counters with a diner nearby which he says is not so noisy. I accede and off I go.

"I gather you don't have a wife?" I ask Jack while we're waiting for our drinks. I hadn't been interested in inquiring before, barely am now, but one must talk small sometimes.

"A life?"

Can't restaurants muffle the noise? Nobody wants to shout at mealtime, but everyone ends up doing it to be heard over everyone else.

"Wuh-wife, Jack. Girlfriend. Partner. Someone with whom a man like you would normally spend this Saturday evening, snuggled up by a warm crackling fire against the cool autumn evening."

"Pretty picture," Jack says, "but, in a word, no. Or in another word, two, but they're both exes. I do snuggle with exes and wives now and then, but they're never mine."

"Poor you," I say without sympathy.

"Hey now. I've earned my sour outlook on matters matrimonial and conjugal."

"I didn't mean to imply that you hadn't. I'm admiring it, that's all."

"And you?" he asks.

"You know the answer to that: I have no significant other. I water the spider plant when she droops. Other than that, no living thing shares my domicile."

"Sounds wonderful. Did you ever?"

"Did I ever what?"

"You know, share your domicile with...anyone?"

"Not going there. I'm in a rosy mood tonight, Jack. See, there are apples in my cheeks and here: I have apples for you."

They're in a cute little paper bag with paper handles, fresh from the Valley. "I'm all about living in the moment. I'm here today and I'll be gone tomorrow, or soon, on some uber-luxury ship that will have more staff than passengers. There'll be someone to carry out the onerous task of turning down my coverlet at night, another dutiful servant to lay the chocolate truffle on the pillow just so, and the Captain to watch over me. That's how I want to share my domicile from here on out. My spider plant may thirst a bit while I'm away, but she has always revived with the application of water when I return."

Our wine, a modest red. comes in tumblers. That's supposed to be chic.

"To hedonism," I toast.

"Aye to that."

"So, what's new, Jack?" I usually don't ask that question, but I know I'll get the news anyway when it comes to Jack.

"I'm thinking of cashing out, Laura, and wanted to consult with you about it. You have a good head on your shoulders and I need to talk this over with a straight-shooter."

I don't acknowledge the character assessment. Compliments such as this usually precede a request.

"Cashing out what—to where?"

"My business. Selling out to my partner. It will come as no surprise to you that the economy tanked, and will likely stay sunk for a good long while. The old days of lighting our cigars with big bills are gone. The cigars are gone. The dancing girls have left our laps and the party's over. In my business, we ride on the backs of our clients in multiples of their success. When they do well, we roll. When they tighten their belts, we don't eat. At all. I could hang in and watch my iceberg of equity shrink to an ice-cube, or I could get out now and still skate a bit. What do you think?"

A career in Decision Support has trained me, first, to carefully select the question; second, painstakingly establish the research criteria; third, meticulously assemble the data; and fourth, thoroughly analyze whether numbers three and two properly answer number one. That's the science.

Once a decision is indicated, then you decide if you like it. If you do, you have your justifications all worked out. If you don't, you change the question or forget you ever asked it. That's the art.

It's similar to using a Ouija board or tossing a coin, but with more paper.

People resist doing things they don't want to do. That's human nature. We just keep procrastinating until we can validate what we want. The thing is, most people aren't aware that we already have our own innate Decision Support system. It's called gut feeling.

So I ask Jack my Golden Question, the one that statistical probabilities cannot answer. "How do you feel about it, Jack?"

"I think it's the right thing to do," he says, unaware of my hand-back. "Like you, I've earned a few dollars, though I see precious little of them because I'm mailing out alimony cheques to a growing list of subscribers, but at least nobody's making me buy expensive towels for the bathroom now. But for work, I could explore other options, maybe have some fun in the process."

"Want to reveal what 'fun' might mean to you?"

"Well, yes I do. Which is where you come in."

"Me? You want me to help you pick out towels?"

"Geez, Laura. I mean—oh, you're kidding, right? No, not towels. Listen. I want to try something, a new twist on an old theme, as it were. Now, hear me out, okay? It's...well, it's the Bo Peep thing."

"Oh, please, Jack, do go on. I wouldn't know what we'd talk about if it wasn't that damn nursery rhyme. First, I'd better have another glass—no, better order me a coffee. I don't want to leave my car in this parking lot overnight."

"Hey, Laura, that's commendable—about the wine, I mean. But listen. These dinner theatres, murder mysteries and all that, they're theatrical productions, you know, written, produced, and copyrighted and all that. But ours, as we've done it a couple times now, this has all the earmarks of a successful show which we could produce or license to other venues. Based on the success we had at the United Way, we wouldn't be starting from scratch. I've already made some inquiries. I've been involved in a few theatre productions—nothing huge—but I really enjoy dinner theatres and we—my exes and I—we used to go to them quite a lot. Lots of fun."

"Well, break a leg and all that," I say. "I hesitate to remind you but I know it will come up: you said I come in somewhere, so why don't you tell me where and end this terrible suspense? I frankly don't see any entrance that I would like to make. Just an exit."

"Oh, no-no-no, I need you in this, don't you see, Laura? Forget that silly 1952 production. The version playing in this new century is of your making, do you realize that? I didn't write any of the, uh, the sermon, I just marshalled the forces around you. You've created the book, as they say in showbiz, and tailored it perfectly for each audience. Let me tell you, I don't know anyone who could deliver as serious a talk as you gave—twice, now—and keep a rowdy, drinking crowd's attention like you did. Really."

The waitress comes for dessert orders. Other than 'Coffee, black', I'm not saying a word.

"Really," Jack repeats. He draws a breath to continue but I raise my hand.

"Shush," I say. "I'm thinking."

I'm not thinking, I'm watching my life flash before my eyes, like I'm falling off a cliff.

I'm retired, well-off, free of encumbrances. I'm looking forward to a life of travel—or am I? Living out of a suitcase, even on a luxury liner, is not my idea of a life, not all the time, anyway. I knew I wanted to retire from my career, but I hadn't considered that I might do different work, because I had no concept of what that might be.

Until this moment.

Whenever I had faced the desire to make a quick and rash decision in my adult life, I held my breath to see if it went away. Other than the daily rash decision to stop at the bar at the Willow Tree corner, that is, but that wasn't made quickly. Since I'm not working now, the bar isn't such a necessary stop on my way home after twelve hours of nonsense. I'm no saint, nor a self-help guru, but I almost never drink at home and I'm not now motivated to get dressed in a power suit just to go over to the bar alone.

Oddly, what Jack is talking about sounds like fun to me. I *was* good at it—the second Bo Peep event more than the first, of course: better costume, better flock of sheep, great audience, slightly better bar. I do possess a sense of humour, or irony, or farce, and I think I can be humorous. When I projected a loving, *laissez-faire* fairy godmother demeanour while standing in a huge gown in front of five hundred United Way donors, *that* was funny. I can't think of another 'celebrity' who would've done it so boldly. Now that I've nothing to lose, no career interest in pre-serving my reputation, I might have something to gain from venturing into a new arena.

"Okay," I say. "I'm in. When do we start?"

Jack blows his coffee half-way across the table. The man has no self-control. "What? You—you're in? But, but I haven't told you yet what I plan to do, my—"

"If we're going to work together, we'll plan together. Won't we, Jack."

This is not a question. Jack coughs and laughs and rolls his eyes. "You take the cake, Laura, you really do. Wow."

"Oh, you have no idea what I take," I say.

+++

Creating our simple dinner theatre production is com-plicated and fractious, as it involves the irresistible force that is Jack Beaufort and the immovable object that is me.

Jack appears to have left his ad agency. He doesn't bring the subject up again and I don't ask, but he seems to have lots of time available for this new project. We form PeepBo Productions Inc. and begin work right away. I do most of the writing—the "creative" as Jack calls it—and he looks after the producing.

Jack has connections everywhere, divided into two camps: those whom he owes, and those who owe him. He offers whichever group he's talking to the same 'opportunity'.

Jack gets us an opportunity to test the show for a two-day engagement at an established downtown dinner theatre location—right after Christmas, of all the luck, a time when people will go to anything, anywhere, just to get out of the house with their holiday guests. But it's not dinner theatre—it's brunch. We haven't done this in front of an audience not inspired by alcohol.

It goes so-so. We should have foreseen that holiday brunchers would have both children and elders with them, and farce is tough for those demographics. Children haven't developed their more sophisticated sense of humour yet, and the white-hairs in the audience seem to have lost theirs, or their hearing, we aren't sure which. Nonetheless, due to the season, we break even.

+++

"Okay, let's get serious," Jack says, rubbing his hands together in a 'getting serious' pantomime.

We're in my living room. It feels odd, as I have so few visitors at my condo. Most of my furnishings are in place to serve a function. That function was, for many years, to get me out to work and support me when I returned. The front wall is all glass, facing southeast overlooking the

Commons, so the view is always up to date. But now, as I watch someone else looking around my home, I see that things are spare, sparse, Spartan. And not in a good way.

"So I reviewed the Customer Feedback cards people left on their tables," Jack is saying. "I didn't know what to make of them at first, but I think there's an interesting trend. See here."

Jack has made a graph. At a glance I can see that it is balderdash.

"Give me those," I say, taking the bundle of cards from the table. "What question did you want answered?"

"What they liked best, second best and so on. Why?"

"That's not what you wanted to know, Jack. You wanted to know *if* they liked the experience. How they *felt* being there. Would they come *back*. Yours are circular questions."

"Circular what? I don't get it."

"Of course you don't, but I will teach you, grasshopper. For instance, look about you, here in my living room. The interior decorator is coming next week to start the upgrades, by the way, but please disregard that and look around. Now, if I ask you to list which piece of furniture you like most and least, what have I done?"

"Um, you've asked me to...to rate your furniture?"

"Yes, good, and in relation to what?"

"In relation to—in relation to the other pieces of furniture?"

"Exactly. And after you have done that, what will I know about how you feel being here?"

Jack's eyes examine the ceiling as he processes the question. "Nothing? You will know nothing."

"Boom!"

"Wow! Laura, I've been in the survey business for years, charged a lot of money doing it, too. Can I please start over? And will you work for me? I mean, with me?"

"Nope, not working for or with anyone, not for pay. Only for my amusement. So far, PeepBo is still amusing, by a slim margin, so let's stick to that. So, where are we?"

"Nowhere," Jack sighs. "I should have gotten you to do these stupid questionnaires."

"Oh, despair not. Let us meditate upon these Tarot cards one by one and see if we can discern what the respondent's true feelings and interests are as we go along. Maybe they have told us more than just whether they prefer Belgian waffles or eggs Benedict."

+++

How do you make a small fortune in business? Invest a large one.

I didn't make that up, but I experienced it.

Actually, we're not losing money but it feels like we should be, if that makes sense. We're spending money on things our customers say they don't want, even as attendance and revenue increase. We're active and engaged and all that, and we argue like we're family. The money flows but its source is a mystery.

We keep changing the product. This is not necessarily a bad thing in show business. The changes are based on our much-better-worded customer feedback cards, which nearly all attendees hand in as they exit, in exchange for a free chocolate truffle.

The customers are not telling us to give them less farce and more or better food. We expected they would, and we double-check when the trend seems to be for less food and more farce—or that's what we interpreted "longer speech" to mean, written under "Other" on so many of the cards. They want less food to eat and more food for thought. They like the band and the singers we hired—and me—but they want us to perform "straight" and not ham it up.

When you're producing a farce with a meal and the audience tells you to get serious and cut the food, but they keep coming anyway, what are you to think? Is that success? And another thing: we have a higher rate of repeat customers than we expected, and higher than any of Jack's ad agency's former restaurant clients ever had. Our ratings are confounding my Decision Support expertise and Jack's Customer Satisfaction experience, too.

We keep the show at brunch-time because there isn't any theatre competition for the time slot, and we continue at the established locale, which keeps them happy with extra revenue. We try moving up to lunchtime, but people want it earlier than lunch, maybe earlier than brunch, maybe breakfast.

Not-funny farce at eight o'clock in the morning? And no food, just coffee, maybe with biscotti? I'm stumped.

We run the show as is, once a week for three months. People have to make reservations weeks ahead to get a seat. Some have reserved the whole run.

Then we take a spring break, meaning that I embark on a Caribbean cruise and Jack goes off to conduct 're-search'. Things have gotten quite testy between us, so the hiatus is welcome.

I plan to get full value from my upper-deck cabin with balcony, the bars, dining rooms, spas and other amenities the ship and ports of call have to offer. If I find myself thinking at all, and I plan to avoid it, I'll ask myself how I went from top civil servant to rank amateur actor in a one-trick pony production that attracts customers even while they tell us they don't like it.

And I will ask myself when I plan to move on to activities more suited to my temperament.

Jan Fancy Hull

Leave them alone

I'm back from my cruise. It's springtime in Nova Scotia, which is to say cold, damp and dull as old pewter, not bright and stunningly beautiful as was the Caribbean. The coldest and dampest part of the whole province seems to be right inside my condo.

While I await the resurrection of my spider plant following her last-rites anointing with water and some plant food for good measure, I look at my walls and the drapes hanging at my floor-to-ceiling plate glass window. It was the best I could afford when I moved in and furnished it, and how many years ago was that? And what mood must I have been in to bring in such cold, unyielding items? Minimalist is a style I admire, but this is not style, it is distinct lack of style. The piano bar aboard *The Queen of Mermaids*, now that was style. Okay, so I'm not living in a *grande salle de luxe*, but my home could look less like a—a what?

Good God. My home is furnished like an executive office in the provincial civil service. Like mine was.

I'm shocked. How did this happen? When one is focused, dedicated, driven—all the traits one is encouraged to have and praised for being during one's climb up the career ladder—one may not notice when the softer attributes fall by the wayside like so many leaves falling, windows closing, roads not taken.

I used to love bright colours, warm breezes, soft conversations. When was that? And now I see I have none of that in my surroundings. Maybe it evolved because I spent all my time at the office. Maybe I didn't mind being away from home so much because both places looked the same.

I had lied to Jack when I told him months ago that the interior decorator would be in that following week, but I'm ready to turn that lie into truth just as soon as the city's decorators get to their offices the next morning. I feel like Scrooge on Christmas Day. Scrooge and I both know you can fix most things as long as you have an epiphany, and money.

The expressions on the faces of decorator candidates parading through my condo with their fabric and paint swatches do not discourage me. The more they wrinkle their pretty little designer noses, the more I think how smart I was to finally recognize the atrocity myself. Three of them endeavour to get me to tell them what I want, which I do not. Two offer ideas of their own, one dull and the other outrageous. One asks not why I want the changes made or how, but why now, especially. So I describe my homecoming from the cruise, the shock following the beauty I so recently had left behind, and I cannot prevent my eyes from welling up as I speak. This lovely person says not a word, but listens carefully, nodding with what I hope is understanding, rather than pity for an eccentric barely in control of her emotions. An eccentric with resources to pay for a very large makeover.

She gets the job, of course, and when she returns with her sketches and samples I am both frightened at the changes and comforted by her calm assurance that I will be very happy in it. Well, what's the worst that can happen? Paint can be re-painted, furniture can be returned. I sure as hell don't like my own decorating choices, so I go with hers.

I'm not the least bit interested in living in the renovation mess. I would loathe getting up and dressed in time for an assortment of painters and delivery men to traipse through my place early every morning, and cleaning up after them every evening. I take a room at the Willow Tree hotel for the duration.

Yes, the hotel housing the wine bar where I received my daily medication for so many years. Well, what's wrong with that? It's handy the condo, so when the designer calls me to select this or approve that, I can pop right over. The dining room is acceptable, sometimes even good. And I do like the bar.

Huston is very solicitous of me. He had thought something bad had happened to me or that I was unhappy with him due to my sudden and prolonged disappearance. Sobriety can strike a bar's patrons without warning, and their loss can be sudden and permanent, though it is rarely contagious. People can and do recover from it. I confess that I have my own temporary recovery from sobriety my first night in the hotel, old habits hardly dying. Without the adrenaline of girding my loins for work at six the next morning, though, the waking up is not so much fun.

+++

Yes, of course I had checked my phone messages when I returned from the trip. Yes, Jack had called—multiple times—but he hadn't left any message and the last call was two weeks before I came home. Once I got involved in the interior makeover whirlwind I forgot all about Jack and the PeepBo conundrum.

After my career of being in constant contact with my masters and minions, I want none of that now. I rarely carry a phone with me, though I made an exception during the renovations. I rarely check my email. Who would I hear from? The Retired Civil Servants' Association? Please.

So I am just back in my new and glorious home, with the warm comfort and elegance of the tropics visible no matter where I look, when the phone rings, and yes, it is Jack Beaufort.

A self-help guru whose book I chanced to read years ago, when my own self needed a lot of help to stay ahead of the game, conjectured that our soul-mate might not be the person who quickens the pulse nor the person with whom we can relax and let down defences. He suggested our soul-mate is someone who challenges us to act above our first instinct. It may be a loved one, but might also be someone whose very presence irritates, thus requiring us to practice the high qualities of patience and forbearance to resist smacking them upside the head. It's a thought. It carried me through several Premiers, Ministers and Deputies. I'm reminded of it now, hearing from Jack.

He is spitting and sputtering in frustration that he hasn't been able to reach me, babbling about startling new developments that will blow this and that thing out of the water.

You know, in my old surroundings, I may have allowed him to come right on over. A home that is furnished like an office will lead you to think that's the efficient thing to do. But in my new surroundings, *manana* is what comes to my mind. I want to soak in my new environment, figuratively and literally, as I have a new tub with jets, and I plan to enjoy it all in peace, with a lovely bottle of bubbly to boot. Even though there is a chilly fog lurking outside, my new lighting makes it seem like a perpetual sunny day inside.

So I tell Jack I cannot see him for two days, and I don't relent when he protests. That's how a place that is furnished like a tropical garden will lead you to think.

Blowing things out of the water is so last year.

+++

It's mid-afternoon when Jack comes up. The real sun is shining, finally, illuminating the new interior. Jack is stunned by it.

"Geez, Laura, I had no idea this was possible," he says. "Are you sure this is the same apartment? It must have cost a small fortune, if you'll pardon my being so middle class in the midst of this sublime luxury."

"Pardon granted. You don't get this sublime luxury without spending a fortune, and note I dropped your modifying diminutive. I had a choice: buy one of those small beachy islands in the Caribbean where royalty and rock stars do drugs, or re-do my condo. The latter seemed the less expensive option at the time, though I'm not sure now. I like it, though."

"I guess you would," Jack says. "And here I was complaining about new bath towels. I am a cheap bugger. No wonder they all left me. Tell me, is there hope for me? Can you teach me to spend my money so women will love me?"

"An amusing thought, but no. I will tell you, though, that this woman—a retired single woman of a certain age, with champagne tastes while living on a meagre government pension—needs you to stop spending her money for her. I still won't love you, but I'll mind you less or even like you a little better if you do. PeepBo Productions has got to get focused *pronto* or be gone. Get me?"

Jack attempts to lean forward to a more businesslike posture in my new armchair, which position that chair is designed to resist. "Laura, since we took our break, I've been doing a lot of research. A lot. I've gone to every dinner theatre and murder mystery train I could find between here and, well, far. I'll fill in the details as I go along. Suffice it to say I have asked new and multiple questions—as you taught me to do, O great mentor—and I have found some astounding answers. Astounding."

"Astound me too, then," I say, amused by his gravity. "Please continue."

"Okay. You recall that we were getting puzzling feedback from our customers, wanting less food, more talk, right?"

"I recall that very clearly, yes."

"And you recall that they wanted the content to be less farce and more serious?"

"Clear as a bell. Clear as mud."

"Right. So first I went to Toronto and took in some of the long-standing dinner theatres there."

"Toronto. My goodness."

"Yeah, I know, but I was determined to find the answer, Laura. Anyway, they all featured variations on food and farce. And music. We weren't off the mark there."

"So, you're getting tired of cheap steak, cheesecake, slapstick and bad songs by this time, I imagine. How did this lead to your astonishment?"

"It wasn't leading to anything we didn't know already. So, I tried a different approach, different questions."

"Oh, good and faithful student," I say. "If I had had you on my staff I might still be working, and governments might be making better decisions this very day. But that water did not flow under my bridge."

"Yeah, or you could've made a bundle for my clients in the crazy world of persuasion. We coulda used you...but here's the thing: instead of investigating what people want at a dinner theatre, I began to look at why people go out at all, anywhere, where they congregate and why, what attracts them. Get it?"

"Yes, maybe. 'Where do people go?' instead of 'why do they go *here*?' And what did you find, Jack? Are we getting to that?"

I mind his step-by-step story-telling. Usually Jack blurts everything. He ignores my push. "I made a list of all the places I could think of that people go, in groups or crowds. It's pretty funny when you read it. Here's my list."

His list is written on stationery from a hotel in New Jersey.

"Atlantic City, Jack? Do they have dinner-theatre casinos, by chance?"

He ignores that, too, so I read the list:

Groups	Why go
Bus	To go places
Sports arena	Watch games
School	Attend / learn
Restaurant	Eat / dine / visit
Circus	See show
Concert	See show
Dinner theatre	See show / eat
Museum	See things / learn
Casino / race track	Gamble

The bottom of the page is torn off. I see nothing astounding in the list and draw no conclusions from it. I hand it back to Jack. "And so?"

"And so, up to that point, I was getting nowhere," he says. "Then I thought of one more place where people go in groups, and I had my 'aha' moment. See here."

He hands me the rest of the page. I read:

Church	Listen / learn / meditate / fit in / get inspired, motivated / be with like-minded people / feel good / be absolved / sing / donate / contribute / join / worship

"Well, well," I say. "Who knew that people attended church for all these reasons, and only went to restaurants to 'eat'? Or to the circus to 'see show'? I see you managed to remember 'worship' at the end of the church list. Do you think maybe you have skewed the reasons some-what?"

"No-no-no, Laura, hear me out. When I got to 'church', the pennies all dropped."

"Maybe that was casino tokens. Or you robbed the collection plate?"

"Funny. Listen. I was stone-cold sober, I assure you. It just made sense. Still does. Church. That's where people go to get what our customers were asking us for: less food, no farce, more serious talk. Several comment cards we got said they'd like to be able to talk to the other customers after the show—remember that? And they kept coming back to hear what you would say the next week, even if it was the same message. Think about it."

"Church?"

"Church."

"Jack, what on earth are you going on about? What—how am I to think about church? 'More fibre, less carbs'? You want us to run a church now? You think I'm a preacher? I studied English, remember? Not theology. The closest I ever came to divinity was fudge. You're out of your cotton-pickin' mind, Jacko. In case you haven't noticed, Mister Market Awareness, churches are waning in popularity, not growing. They would definitely not show up on anyone's list as a good investment or hobby—which is the door I came in, by the way, hobby. I'm not the least bit interested in participating in any born-again enterprise, Jack—surely you know that, and Little Bo Peep will not find me inside any church!"

I take a deep breath and continue. "I think you and I had better come to terms we can deal with, right here and right now. I thought about this a lot while I was away, and now I've decided. It's been a slice, but as of now, I'm out. In fact, I am so out that you can have my share of the business free and clear. I'll call my lawyer tomorrow and get the papers drawn up. No debate and no hard feelings."

I stand up. "Now, can I make you a cup of tea, Jack?"

I have to say, I am gob-smacked at where Jack has gone, but relieved at the same time. I did give our theatre project a little thought while I was away, of course, and had concluded that my retirement destiny was not to be an actress, nor to be Jack's business partner. The Bo Peep game had served its purpose as a break from the civil ser-vice for me, period. If the audience prefers a deeper nu-ance, a motivational inclination, something inspirational, I'm not their girl, definitely not their guru. Jack has opened a door I can exit through, with cause, and I take it.

While I prepare tea—my mid-afternoon souvenir from the cruise—there is no conversation, the first time there hasn't been constant chatter from Jack. This is my version of high tea, with scones and jam, though no cream. I've begun to exhume my bones through better diet and daily walks around the Common and I don't want to re-inter them under clotted cream.

"Laura, can I ask you something?" Jack says after de-claring his appreciation of the scones, which I am proud to say I made myself.

"That question usually precedes an uncomfortable conversation, but we've already had it, so rush in, fool."

"Okay, I will. Listen. uh, do you believe in, uh, anything? I mean, like, do you have—this sounds so hokey—do you have faith? Like, in...in something bigger? In a higher be-ing?"

"My goodness, Jack, I once had faith in your ability to say whatever was on your mind, but I'm beginning to lose it. Spit it out, man. Do I have faith, as in Father, Son and Holy Ghost and all those fellows? As in organized reli-gion? Do I believe in God? Is that your question?"

"Yeah, that's my question. If you don't mind. I know it's none of my business."

"You're right, it's not, but I'm in a hot buttered mood right now so I'll let you in on my little secret. No."

"No faith?"

"No."

"Atheist, then?"

"No, I wouldn't say that. To be an atheist you'd believe that God *doesn't* exist. As opposed to theists who believe that God *does* exist. I'm saying I don't know. Which is the definition of agnostic."

"Were your parents, you know, believers?"

"I'm sure you think I was raised by wolves, but I actually come from a reasonably decent family: one mother, one father, no rival siblings, a few passing benevolent grandparents. My parents were both educated. They expected that I would follow their example, and they supported me in my pursuit of higher learning, where you and I met. They considered many things other than school and university to be part of a well-rounded education, too. From as early as I can remember, we went to the theatre and symphony, and church, too. Sometimes one or the other would take me, sometimes we all went together. We'd attend different churches around town, none regularly, to hear a particular preacher or a choir, and we'd discuss what we saw and heard afterward. It was never assumed that we would go to anything just because it was Sunday morning or Friday night. We never bought season tickets to anything. We would read about something or so-and-so and decide to go. My parents never joined a church, nor did I. So, as far as I know, my parents didn't hold religious faith in the common use of the word. We observed faith, discussed it from time to time, and I understand its appeal a little. How about you, Jack, since Miss Manners dictates that I ask the reciprocal?"

"Me? Nah."

"My, my. Thanks for sharing, Jack."

"Well, let me finish. I'm not a believer, in the church-religion sense of the word, and I don't think I want to be, but I do have questions, you know? I think it'd be nice if there was a place you could go to hear about, you know, those topics, without having someone get you in a half-nelson and make you pray with them until you confess your sins."

"Prayers and rasslin'? Why not? Prayer is part of pro football, it seems, so there's a precedent. So, why are we discussing faith or the absence thereof?"

"The thing is, Laura, the crazy thing is that I think there are a lot of people out there like you and me—very different, but the same, somehow, you know? I'm not saying it very well. I think a lot of people were attracted to our little show and heard something in your monologues that resonated with them, something that maybe reminded them of their formative years in church, before they, uh, drifted away from their faith, if I can put it that way."

"You can put it any way you want. So you're saying that as a result of seeing a Bo Peep farce, people want to go back to church? I'm not sure I agree, but there's still nothing in it for me."

"I want to tell you more about my trip, can I? After my, you know, eye-opener in Atlantic City, I drove down to Florida. If you're looking for oddities, Florida is one place you'll find them. I wanted some warm weather anyway and Florida was in my headlights, so I went to the Sunshine State and observed a few churches."

"You've got to be kidding. Isn't that the big, shiny buckle of the Bible Belt?"

"No, I'm not kidding. It's not the first time I've done market research by going on the road and actually getting a feel for things, breathing the same air, sleeping in the same beds as the customers. Market surveys don't always get the response you need, because people can only answer the questions you ask, as you know better than anyone. You don't know what else to ask because you haven't been on site to see all that goes into an experience."

"I'm impressed with you. So you've been to London to visit the Queen," I say. "And what did you there, pussy-cat? Did you frighten a little mouse under her chair?"

"I know you think it's silly, Laura, but I'm dead serious. Now listen to me, please, with your mind open as wide as it can go. I went to churches in some really poor areas. I was nervous to even drive through."

"My, you will stop at nothing for authenticity in research. Was that necessary?"

"I thought it was. Especially since I didn't know what I was looking for. I also went to modern cathedrals where I thought my good-enough Honda was barely good enough to park in their lots amongst the Jags and Lexuses."

"You did visit the Queen!"

"A bit, yeah. In the poor churches, the preachers preached angry. They preached sin and corruption and repentance and salvation or damnation after death—the damnation mostly for rich folks."

"What you'd expect."

"Right. And in the rich churches, the preachers preached reward, thanksgiving and joy. No mention of corruption or sin or death, certainly not of damnation. Lots of guilt, though."

"It's like picking a TV channel for your news depending on whether you incline to the right or the left."

"Exactly! That's my point, Laura. As little as I knew about church, which was next to zilch, I always thought that they were basically all the same. Oh, I knew that some had women priests and some allowed their priests to marry and all that, but I thought the message was basically the same. Now, as a thinking ad man, I don't know why it had escaped me that all the whaddya-callems—denominations and sects—they all exist because people have preferences, not just in their interpretations of the Bible, but in how they want their church experience to be. What the interior looks like, plain or fancy, what sort of robes the priest or pastor wears or doesn't wear, what kind of music—that's a biggie—what language, how soft or hard the seats are. They basically choose their experience."

"Do they, now? The leaders of these churches—archbishops and popes and rabbis—might have a thing or two to say about that. They don't make wars over seat cushions, Jack. It's over dogma, as I mentioned in one of my monologues, come to think of it. Think of the Spanish Inquisition. They didn't torture people because they disagreed on interior decorations."

"I think you're wrong, Laura. The leaders may well have picked their fights over doctrine, but maybe doctrine's just another word for nothing left to lose."

"What?"

"What I mean is, while the leaders murdered the unbelievers over doctrine, the great unwashed surely weren't able to grasp the finer points, since most couldn't even read in the old days. They just did what they were told because they'd get killed themselves if they didn't. We haven't had a declared religious war on this continent, but people still choose their churches based on a few simple non-religious factors."

"Such as?"

"Upbringing counts for a lot, same as in politics. Stylistic preferences, like music. Services offered, mostly day-care and accessibility, refreshments, parking. Ambience."

"Ambience. You're kidding."

"Am not. Ambience: not just for restaurants anymore." Jack gestures as he speaks, as though tracing the words on a billboard.

"Jack, as a topic of conversation, this is an odd one. As a business discussion, it's off the agenda. Can we adjourn now? I have places to go, exercise to get."

"Okay, sure Laura, but promise me that we can talk about it some more?"

"Not going to make that promise, sorry. I just don't see me in it. If you want to explore your faith or absence thereof, find a shaman or drum circle or priest who is skilled in these matters. I'm not and don't want to be."

I put on my jacket and leave when Jack leaves, just so I won't have told a lie. Any excuse for another walk around the Commons.

When the late spring weather isn't miserable, as I've described, it's glorious. Today it's the latter. A few people —not as many as should be—are walking, some pulled by dogs. You can smell the green grass and the muddy ground. It may sound ugly, but you have to be here to fully appreciate it, and I am here.

I have to say, the new 'me' that is emerging since I retired is someone I am enjoying getting to know. After a career of keeping a tight grip, I'm surprised that I'm remembering how to relax and take a deep breath. Carlos helped me with that. Carlos was the masseur on the cruise. I made good use of him, and he did me a world of good.

Never too late, I say as I stride along. *Never too late.*

+++

I've been to my hairdresser, the Italian deli, the Port of Wines store, and returned with a hairstyle suitable for walking in all weather, plus assorted, over-priced delicacies. The day is too nice to waste, the second warm day in a row. I don't want to stay indoors yet, so I deposit my purchases in my apartment, pick up the keys to my sweet ride and go for a short drive to a large cemetery.

Yes, a graveyard. Most of my known family members lie buried there. They paid for perpetual care, but it's seemly that their only surviving family member should appear at least once a year, so that visitors at their headstones won't only be the people who mow the grass.

I park and start off down a path leading away from the family plot so I can get some walking done first, while getting settled with being in this stunted forest of monuments. I don't believe in the after-life, but these stones are hard evidence of the before-death, and there is a very eclectic group of lives represented here, from victims of the *Titanic* to war dead to paupers to educators, the last including my folk.

Here they are, then, looking much the same, a little lichen growing on the granite. I like what you've done with the place, Pater and Mater. Both were gardeners, but there are no flowers here, live or plastic. Dust to dust is fine. If they'd left it up to me, there mightn't even have been a gravestone, not meaning any disrespect. They made their own arrangements anyway, probably anticipating my bent. After Father died, Mother had both their names and dates engraved on the large stone, leaving only her own final date for me to see to.

Now here's a curious thing I've noticed about myself: whenever there's something in front of me to read, I read it. When there is nothing to read, I'm fidgety. Curiouser still: when there is nothing to read but just a few words, as on a road sign, as often as I read it, I cannot remember it. I read the same signs every time I come across them, but they always read like news, but news I can't remember. It's annoying.

So now I'm reading my parents' tombstone though I have read it hundreds of times before. Well, no. I haven't been here hundreds of times since they died. Dozens. A dozen, then.

Anyway, I'm reading his name, her name, his dates, her dates, and I see a series of letters and numbers at the very bottom of each side, just above the sod. Did I ever see that before? Not that I recall, but that's not proof that they weren't there. I may have forgotten, or they may have been obscured by taller grass before. Perhaps the groundskeepers hadn't trimmed closely around the stone just before my previous visits.

I take my new smart-phone from my bag and photo-graph the codes, just for practice: **PS14:1** under dear old Father's name, and **PS22:20-21** under Mother's. Maybe they are perpetual care codes, indicating that they had paid for the grass to be mowed and no trashy plastic flowers should ever be laid there. I have complied, if so.

Yes, a smart-phone. I was curious about that ubiquit-ous device that everyone seems unable to live without, so one day I inquired. When I left the store, I owned one. Now I'm photographing gravestones with it, feeling just a little creepy.

Also creepy is the extra space beside their graves in the plot. Room for one more, also paid in full. All I'll have to do is slip in when I'm ready, Mother had said with a twinkle in her eye. No room there for anyone to slide in beside me, I've noted. I guess she had figured that wouldn't be required.

+++

I'm at my lawyer's office, reviewing the papers to sell my shares of PeepBo Productions Inc. to Jack for a dollar. Jack can make lists of reasons people assemble in crowds without me. I'm done with it.

My lawyer reaches for my new phone, which I've taken out to show off to her. "Congratulations, Laura! You're not a Luddite after all!" she teases. "Oh, this is the new-new version. May I?"

She swipes her manicured finger at the icons on the screen with the speed of familiarity, something I suppose I will be able to do eventually.

"Oh, by the way, since you're off the clock," I say pointedly, "take a look at this photo. Do you recognize this code? It's on my parents' gravestone, just noticed it, thought I'd check it out. My guess is a monument company engraver's code or instructions to the graveyard-keeper?"

She glances at the letters and numbers in the photo and then hands the phone back to me with a level look. "You're not serious."

"Yes, why? What?"

"You may not be a Luddite, but I can see that you're a heathen."

"'Scuse me? Upon what evidence do you base this charge?"

"Laura, my dear, think: besides names and dates, what do you find on headstones?"

"Moss? The only tombstone I'm in the habit of reading in any detail is the one under which the ashes of my dearly departed now lie. You evidently have seen lots of them, probably required reading in law school. So, share the wisdom, please."

"P-S-one-four-colon-one, my friend, means the Book of Psalms, chapter fourteen, verse one. The other is Psalm twenty-two, verses twenty and twenty-one. "

"Not Bible verses. No way."

"Yes way. Bible verses. Commonly found on head-stones. A final statement of faith by the deceased on their way to their reward. You were not aware of this inscription before?"

I explain my groundskeeper-grass theory, thank her and leave. I want to ask her to show me the verses, as I am certain any law firm that charges as much as hers does would have several very nice Bibles in their library, but I'm afraid the extra fifteen minutes that would take would find their way on a bill sometime, and I don't want to pay money for my ignorance.

As I drive home I'm feeling out of sorts. How *could* they? My parents, I mean. Bible verses on their head-stones? Psalms? I thought the Psalms were songs of praise. To God. Were my parents believers behind my back? That sounds intolerant. Am I intolerant? Of course not. What, then?

Did they think they should hide their faith from me? Did they think I would mock them? I might well have, but we often engaged in vigorous discussion on many topics, including politics, the arts, hockey, and religion, and we each did our best to find ways to disagree, just to hone our debating skills. Now I discover this, their final, 'Top this, Laura darling,' but it's too late for me to reply.

You win, Mother and Father, but only by default. Playing after you're dead is cheating, remember that.

I do have a Bible at home, a good one. My interior designer had suggested some "weighty" books would look good on the under-shelves of my side tables, and I told her to select whatever she thought suitable. I hadn't cared what they were or if they were even real books, but during an infrequent dusting I had discovered that one was a Bible, huge, gilt-edged and very heavy. Curious choice, I had thought. By the look of its tooled leather cover and gilt-edged pages, I expect I paid handsomely for it.

I carry it now to my breakfast table to read. It must weigh five pounds, obviously meant for a church lectern. The onionskin pages crackle as I open the cover and find the index. No, I don't know where the Psalms come in the sequence of books. Aren't there sixty-some books in the Bible? Who remembers what they all are and in what sequence? Does anyone recall the order in which Shakespeare wrote his plays? Well, I might, actually, given time.

I read the first Psalm inscription first, the one I photographed beneath my father's name. I'm surprised by it and feel once again left out of something. Then I find the one that was under my mother's name, and am even more puzzled.

Then it dawns on me. They must have *pretended* to follow convention by having those Biblical testimonials inscribed in stone. Maybe they were offered at no extra charge, so they used them to take one of their favourite debates to the grave where it could be waged for eternity, as it were. I can hear them laughing about it, my father wheezing through his oxygen mask.

Here they are:

> Father's: *Psalm 14:1 – The fool hath said in his heart, There is no God.*

> Mother's: *Psalm 22: 20-21 – Deliver my soul from the sword; my darling from the power of the dog. Save me from the lion's mouth: for thou hast heard me from the horns of the unicorns.*

The power of the dog? Horns of the unicorns? Oh, Mother, laughing last *is* best.

Father had always tended towards the side of the possible rather than the impossible whenever we debated the existence of A Supreme Being, so on his monument he had played his usual hand. Not saying that there *is* a God, just saying it's foolish to say there isn't. I'd heard him say that many times, can hear his voice now. I just didn't know he was quoting scripture.

Mother, on the other hand, preferred joke to argument, so her response is complete nonsense, and fun. Quite likely a poor translation from the original, now a scriptural raspberry. She probably looked up Father's Psalm and then searched nearby for a rebuttal. It's on the opposite page to his in my huge tome. Way to go, Mother!

I'm laughing and my eyes sting with tears. I do miss them.

+++

I have the papers from my lawyer. I want to get them signed and over with so I can move on, though I don't know where 'on' will be yet. Twice-daily walks and after-noon tea don't take up all the time in a day, and I'm not interested in mall-crawling. The United Way has been calling for me to take on a volunteer role, but I want to see what Laura Lloyd, retiree, wants to do before I lend my considerable talents—their words—to the goals of others.

Jack has asked if I can bring the papers to his house. There's no car in his driveway so I pull in.

"Hey, Laura, come in, if you can stand a bachelor pad. Your place is so much nicer."

"We're not in a Better Homes and Gardens competition, Jack. You invited me, so don't apologize for your place now that I'm here."

I look around. His house is a large one-storey bunga-low in the steep hills behind Bedford. There is a partial, distant view of the harbour from the dining-room win-dow. The place is furnished in Early Newlywed style from the nineties, in fair condition. Dated. I can say that, now that my place is no longer Stark Office style.

Jack hangs my coat in the foyer closet, which is other-wise empty. Where I expect the hallway leading to the bedrooms to be, there's a bedsheet tacked across the opening.

"What're you up to, Jack?" I ask. "Doing a little home remodelling?"

"What? Oh, that. Uh, no. It's my practice range. Do you golf?"

"Me? Hell no. No athletic genes in this body, if golfing is considered athletic. What did you say this sheet is for?"

"Ah, well, you see, it's one of the perks of being a bach-elor – nobody to say 'take that damn sheet down and stop swinging that club before you break something.'"

He says this in the voice of an unhappy female.

"You practise golf in here? Pardon me for sounding like the nag you just quoted, but mightn't you break something? Or are you that good?"

"I'm pretty good," he says. "That's what practice is for. The ceilings are high enough."

As he leads me to the dining room I notice several pock-marks in the walls on either side of the sheet but don't mention them.

The table is covered in piles of business documents, with a corner patch cleared for our use. Another perk of being a bachelor, I suppose, but, for once, I resist the urge to comment. I open the envelope and hand Jack the documents, the colourful tags instructing him to "Sign Here" sticking out at various angles.

Jack takes my papers and lays them on the pile without looking at them. I notice several other sets of papers with blue cardboard corners interspersed throughout the pile. Legal documents, ignored. I keep an eye on my set.

"Before we do that," he nods towards my lawyer's handiwork, "I want to show you something pretty interesting. I convinced my former partner to let me dig through our files of existing research, market tests and things like that, and I found a study that the School of Theology had commissioned us to do, not more than ten years ago. See here—"

"Jack," I say as calmly as I can, "I just want to be done with this venture. We agreed that I would sign my shares over to you for one dollar, which I hope you have on you, and then I'm done. It's been a slice, but *sayonara*. Please sign."

I point to my papers, which are in jeopardy of sliding down behind the table.

"Okay, I will, okay? I'll sign your papers. But will you just listen to me, Laura, for a minute? I'll sign. Just listen. Here, can I get you something, a glass of water? I might have a ginger ale."

He goes to the kitchen before I can answer. I hear ice cubes falling into glasses, and then a can hissing open. He brings in a glass for each of us.

"Only had one left, sorry, so we'll share. Cheers."

I don't know what clues me in, maybe that he is un-shaven, that he is irritable, or has no car, or only one can of ginger ale, but I suddenly know Jack is in trouble. "Something wrong, Jack? Are you working? I mean, did the sale of your shares of your business go through? Or fall through?"

Not my business, but it seems relevant at this moment.

"Yes and no to all questions. I'm working a bit on a few faithful accounts, as long as we can hang on to them. Try-ing to deliver the services they've already paid for so we won't have to refund retainers which are long gone. Turns out I was too late thinking about cashing out. There's nothing left. My partner and I both wanted our dividends more than we wanted to survey our own trends, so by the time he and I sat for our chat, we were tits up. Excuse me. We're in receivership now."

"I'm sorry, Jack, that's awful! What—what will you do?"

"I don't know. What would you do? Run away and join the circus? I might as well. My car's been repo'd. I've lost this house, mortgage foreclosed. I have to move out by the end of this month. The good news is that when I'm fi-nally a pauper I can petition to reduce the alimony pay-ments I send to far too many ex-wives."

"I'm not an expert on such matters, but wasn't your company incorporated to limit your liability to business assets for this very situation? Why would you lose your house?"

Jack looks as bleak as I have ever seen anyone look, and in the civil service I've seen some bleak-looking people. "Because we set up a new line of credit to cover the growing cash flow shortage," he says, staring at the tabletop, "and we could only get it on our personal signatures, using our residences as collateral."

"You didn't!" I'm immediately sorry I said it.

"You weren't there. I know it sounds stupid now. It *was* stupid. We just never expected the lights to go out all over town so quickly. We could compete with our competitors, you know? We could go toe-to-toe with the big houses, and often did. But you can't fight against nothing, and that's what sank us: a huge wave of nothing. The arse came right out of her, as the fishermen say. The goddamn recession, it shrank the segment of the economy we were doing business with by about thirty percent. Well, guess where we had been working? On the top ten percent. When that ship hit the sand we were in the cold, cold water. If we had had courage or foresight we should-a could-a would-a pulled the plug when things started getting tight, without taking the stupid step of tossing our homes into the maelstrom."

"Hindsight, Jack. In other circumstances, what you did might have been lauded as moxie."

"Yeah, in other circumstances, sure. Moxie. That's rich. Our clients paid us for the expertise to steer them into good circumstances so they'd stay flush and we'd still be solvent. I just hope they don't sue us for steering them under the waves. Oh, well, what the hell, eh? You're lucky, you have that nice, cushy civil service pension. As long as you don't marry some two-timing loser like me, you're set for life."

Don't I just hate that cushy-pension comment. People don't realize, nor should they, how close our government has come to falling apart from time to time, just as Jack's business is doing, were it not for the heroic efforts of some of its senior civil servants who took our responsibilities personally over the years. If this province is ever sold to a qualified buyer, I'll demand a share of the proceeds. I earned it. There were times, back in the days of a certain premier who shall remain nameless, when you could have sold us all from Yarmouth to Sydney for two dollars, we were so robbed, given away, pork-barrelled, and mismanaged. I earned my pension, every penny of it.

"This is obviously a very bad time for you, Jack," I say, reaching toward the transfer of ownership documents. "Let's just get this done and I'll be out of your hair. The good news is that there is money in the bank account, and it's all yours with this transfer. I hope that helps. Do you have a pen?"

"No. I mean, I can't sign, Laura."

"Why the hell not?"

Jack looks like a dead man. No, a dead man would look happier. "I pledged my share of PeepBo to the bank, too. There's a lien against PeepBo, so now the production company is entangled in the bankruptcy. So that includes you."

I not only dream of murder, I sometimes think of it when I am wide awake, and this is one of those times. A sort of pretend murder, like smacking a heavy crystal ashtray into Jack's skull, but not causing his actual death or injury, just giving me the satisfaction of striking a blow. Thank goodness nobody has crystal ashtrays any more.

"I authorized no loans, no collateral agreements. A lien has no basis." The former Director of Decision Support is speaking.

"No, Laura, I know you didn't." Jack sounds very tired. "But I did, at least my shares. Nowadays, lawyers use the shotgun approach, not a sniper's rifle, and they drag everyone into court and let the judge do the work of sorting out who should be included in the action and who shouldn't. So PeepBo is named in the bankruptcy suit." Jack nods toward the mound of papers on the table. "We can't buy, sell or trade until all that's settled. You'll get official notice on Monday, likely."

"Why wouldn't my lawyer have known this?" The list of people I'd like to use the ashtray on may be growing.

"Paperwork takes time, I guess. It's all very recent. No doubt your lawyer did due diligence on these papers, but meanwhile, across town, someone else was doing mine at the same time. I'm very sorry."

"Sorry doesn't begin to cut it, Jack."

"Well, hey, I get that," he replies, with some heat. "But what difference does it make to you, really? You were about to sign the whole shebang over to me anyway, so what's the big deal? You're out, no matter what. I'll make sure someone lets you know when the way is clear to execute those papers. Meanwhile, don't worry about it. You wanted out, you're out, okay? And there's no need to roll your eyes, Laura. I get it that you're angry."

He has recklessly risked our corporate partnership, such as it was, and my good name, and he finds it in his heart to chastise me because I have rolled my eyes. Honestly, I find it hard not to smack him. Instead, I reach across the table and grab my documents, knocking the rest of the pile to the floor. Jack doesn't even glance at it.

I retrieve my coat from the foyer closet, the wire hanger rattling as it falls to the floor, and leave without another word.

+++

Damn-damn-damn-damn. Every step I take has a swear-word attached to it, and I'm on a long and fast walk so there are lots of thoughts to curse. I'm mad, and angry because I'm mad, and frustrated because I'm angry, and on it goes. And, of course, the list of what's making me angry eventually includes me. Why-why-why-*why* did I ever say I would get involved in that ridiculous venture with that ridiculous man-child, and if I ever thought it was a good idea, why did I have to go and seal it with a legal agreement? The only personal legal agreements I ever signed in my life were my employment contracts and my one mortgage. And my investment documents.

This must be what married couples face when their jig is up. Have I lost my mind, have my well-honed smarts dulled in retirement? I certainly hadn't needed the money, so why had I done it?

Vanity? Hardly. I was the putative 'star' of the show, but I had found it uncomfortable more than ego-boosting.

Well, look at your ego now, Laura Lloyd.

Ah, self-recrimination, the most injurious wound of all. We know where to aim the slings and arrows for maximum damage, and it's too close-range to duck the shot.

Well, bleep Jack Beaufort and his ill-fated schemes. If he drowns in debt I'm sure he's earned every dip beneath the waves—wives, businesses and all. Screw him.

If there is even a shadow of threat to my good name through this affair I'll mount my defence in the usual way —with a blistering offence—and hang what's left of him out on McNab's Island where they used to hang pirates and petty thieves.

I'm sure there's a good show or concert playing in Toronto or New York. Since I've marched myself over to

Spring Garden Road I stop in to see what my travel agent has to sell, and I make a quick selection. Nothing is so bad it can't be run away from. Mother used to say that, sometimes taunting Father, sometimes in her own defence. I'll use it however it works for me.

I visit my lawyer to tell her what's transpired. She purses her lips in a way I can't read, nor do I want to. If her puckering suggests she'll actually have to put her law school education to work, that's too damn bad. I didn't intend to do anything wrong at any time, and surely ignorance *is* an excuse in this situation. For me, I mean, not for Jack.

My advocate promises to "look into it", which isn't as good as promising to make it all go away, but I accept that Rome was built in stages, so off I go, determined to enjoy myself.

+++

"We'll be fine."

My lawyer's assistant called to invite me to her office as soon as I returned from my entertainment tour. I'm kept waiting for an annoying length of time in the firm's reception area, during which I am offered coffee, tea, ice water, sparkling water, juice, and *The Toronto Star*. I half expect the pages of the newspaper to be ironed, the receptionist is so formal and deferential.

I am finally sitting in my lawyer's office, where I feel I personally paid for the various *objets d'art* on her credenza. And the credenza.

"Just stay out of it, is my advice," she says. "I've written a letter to the court to clarify and solidify our position. Due process will resolve everything. We won't be harmed in any way. I've re-sent the partnership termination papers to his law firm and they will see that they are signed in due course."

The reason I have kept this advocate is that she uses inclusive language like "our position". I'll never be in legal poop alone, and that's a happiness money can buy.

I've calmed down after showing myself a good time in the big city and therefore resist the urge to ask if there's anything "we" can do to further censure Jack. I don't want my lawyer's condescending reprimand. Jack is being censured enough through his own efforts.

Jan Fancy Hull

And they will come home

About two years later

They say it's not good for your health to have nothing to occupy your mind, but I sometimes wonder if being this busy is healthy, either.

I know the answer to that. My health has never been better, according to the youngster who poses as a doctor, my 'family physician' as her receptionist refers to her. I go to her because my old doc retired—none too soon—and I found this new kid nearby, which was a lucky break, as there is a critical shortage of doctors hereabouts. She can't be old enough to have a degree in medicine, though her sheepskin is on the wall. I made sure I saw it.

I must seem ancient to her. Archaeological, even, a glacial anomaly in a waiting-room full of smooth-skinned young mothers and their babies. But, bless her heart, she says she's unearthed a good artifact in me. She sure was keen on the dig. She poked and prodded and ordered tests for things I didn't know people could have, healthy or ill, some of them quite common in "people my age", she said. My liver—about which I'd had some secret concerns based on what and how I fed it for so long—didn't even merit a comment. My blood pressure was mentioned sternly, *and* cholesterol, but they're so fussy about those things these days. It's a sign of a healthy population, if you ask me, when they lower thresholds to capture new patients. Anyhow, I rejected any discussion of medications, which pleased her, and that pleased me, so "we" are still exercising and watching "our" diet.

Do they teach that language in medical and law and dental schools now, using the first person plural instead of the second person singular? Do I feel more comforted when my professionals say "we"? It doesn't bother me; it just amuses me. I know they're patronizing me, but why not let them, the dears?

The United Way had wanted me to join in the annual campaign for some time. I had avoided replying until after Jack and I split up, and if that sounds like the end of a relationship between Jack and me, so be it. There were strong feelings of betrayal on my part, plus embarrassment for being involved with him at all. I'm sure many ex-couples can relate.

The United Way was a good antidote. I was very impressed with the quality of the citizenry, including a large contingent of the military, who were committed to the project. Some of them I had known professionally over many years. I had made some contributions to past campaigns from time to time, of course, and loaned my staff when it was feasible. And there was that silly gala, making me a certified minor celebrity. How could I say I was too busy in retirement when these people are running business, church, and state, and still offering to help?

Charitable deeds may seem out of character for me. Some people live their lives widely, doing a bit of everything as they go along. Professor MacArthur comes to mind as an example of this. I'm not one of those people, it seems. My life might be described as narrow, linear; which is to say I did one thing at a time, and career was first. It may be a risky way to go about things, as one's lifeline might end without notice and then one's other potentialities might not get attempted.

But so what? I'm not here for the record. I'm not in a competition, and not concerned about my legacy. I just want to escape the lion's mouth as well as I can, to paraphrase Mother's gravestone inscription. Someone else can blow the unicorn's horn.

It was my chosen path to be a civil servant for those many years, which called upon all my resources to serve the public. Now, I want to see what I can do to serve me. Different tasks require one to exercise different parts of one's head, heart and hands. That puts one on the down-sloping side of the fabled learning curve for a while, but I'm not afraid of that. I've already suffered embarrassment—not getting that promotion, and the Bo Peep fiasco—and survived. I've plenty of income no matter what I do, thanks to my canny investments from an early age and my satisfactory pension.

So working for charity is not a stretch now. And working when you don't have the lurching ox-team of ambition and income steering your every decision is quite liberating. I recommend it.

+++

I'm at the Lieutenant Governor's mansion, attending a posh *soiree* put on to thank this year's significant United Way donors and volunteers, of which I seem to be both. It's shameful how little one can give to charities in this city and be considered a major philanthropist. My investor's brow furrowed at the amount of funds I wanted to donate, but she made it work.

Anyway, it's a splendid, low-cost affair, with community-college hospitality students at my left elbow offering faux champagne in flutes, and catering students at my right elbow with trays of really very tasty savouries. Students from the Conservatory are playing music in the historic residence's elegant ballrooms. I'm enjoying one-minute conversations with just about everyone there, many of whom I know and others who look interesting enough to meet. How's that for coming out of my shell?

I move from one ballroom, where a ten-year-old boy is astounding us on the grand piano, to another in which two girls are playing amazingly complex music on violins. Standing out in this ornate room of dark-suited pale-skinned men—including men whose skin colour was never pale, of course, but who have the pallor of too-much-rainy-weather about them as well—is a tall, trim, man in a light silk designer suit, with glowing skin that has recently been under warm sun, hair tastefully greying at the temples and a salt and pepper beard nicely trimmed, if you like that sort of thing. He has the bearing of a movie star, from the back, at least.

I decide I shall sidle over near him to add some in-terest to my meeting and greeting. As I make my way to-ward him, he turns and sees me just as I recognize him to be Jack Beaufort.

"Oh, shit", I say under my breath. At least, I hope it's under. I've been easily well-mannered for many months, but here's Jack and I'm struggling.

Soul-mate indeed.

"Oh, Laura, good! There you are!" Jack says over the chatter and music, and I'm trapped.

I wonder what excuse I can make to avoid him as he excuses his way through the crowd toward me, but there is no hasty escape. I would merely get caught in the line-up at the exit, where the red-serged Mounties are waiting to retrieve our coats and respectfully bid us *bon soir*.

"Hello, Jack," I say, with no warmth. "Been away?"

"Away and back many times, actually. Just got in on the weekend and I'll be going again soon."

Jack takes my elbow, rotates us away from a noisy knot of volunteers, and bends close.

"Laura, I was hoping to meet you here," he says quietly. "I know you've been ignoring my calls and I don't blame you. Not at all. The way things went down between us, well, I'm really very sorry about all of it. I should never have involved you in my troubles. I was greedy and thoughtless and I sincerely apologize."

I look at Jack in disbelief. This is a textbook confession of fault and apology without excuse. Further, he hasn't immediately begged for forgiveness. This is so unlike the facile and quarrelsome Jack of my previous acquaintance. I'm speechless. And more than a little suspicious.

"I'm sure you're uncomfortable seeing me right now, Laura, but I wonder if you would sit with me for a moment? There is something more I'd like you to know. I think you'll be interested. And don't worry, I won't try to hustle you."

Zounds! Has he learned mind-reading, or taken sensitivity training as part of a community-service sentence? I'm sitting on one of the Lieutenant-Governor's antique settees with him before I know what's happened. I've still not spoken.

"Thanks, Laura," he says, leaning in towards me just a bit as we sit. His cologne is unlike any others I have sampled at this reception in that it smells expensive, and very good.

"I have so much good news to tell you. For example, I want you to know that I'm making full financial restitution to both my exes, including child support, and then some."

"Child—you had children?"

"A child, yes. I had—have—a daughter. She's graduating from high school this year. I've gotten to know her a little better recently, but these things take time. I assure you that I'm not telling you this so you'll think I'm a good person. But it's important to me that you know I've really changed. I hurt a lot of people in my past, and I want to make amends. When I went bankrupt, I hit bottom and felt, uh, felt sorry for myself for a time. It wasn't pretty. But then I got involved with some powerful people, did some powerful thinking and encountered some powerful good fortune. But I was still miserable. I realized that the only way I could really start to feel better was to repair the damage I had caused to the people I cared about. If they would let me."

Jack breathes a big sigh. I don't know if I want to hear this story or not. It's uncomfortable watching a villain try to redeem himself before my very eyes. He can reform all he wants on his own time, but I feel a resistance to changing my opinion of him on short notice. I'm on the lookout for flaws even more than is my wont, for clues that he's just blowing more smoke. My expression doesn't hide that.

"You see, Laura, I've made a very large amount of money in a very short time, and I stand to make a lot more. All legal. But that proverbial ship can run aground at any time, as we all know, so while I have the opportunity, I've been making restitution. Besides my misusing my friends and family over the years, all kinds of other people got shafted when I went bankrupt. They didn't deserve that from me. They all worked for me or with me in good faith. I'll pay them all back. Including the government—my tax accountant and lawyer are looking into that for me. I'll pay just what I owe there, though. I'm not going for sainthood."

That's something, a little clue, not that Jack is faking but that he hasn't turned born-again perfect. That's a relief. Perfection is a confection, like that awful edible-oil whipped-cream substitute, formless, tasteless, ready to dissolve as soon as there's any heat.

"So," Jack continues, "I am also indebted to you, Laura. No, please, let me say this. You gave me your shares and assets of PeepBo, which I appreciated, believe me. I was able to get out of town with the final bit of cash from that bank account, to lie low for a bit. Turns out where I decided to hole up was where I found my new calling, as it were. You incurred legal costs in preparing that transfer of ownership and I will repay them."

Still no 'gotcha' from Jack. I'm so primed for it that I can't help myself. "Where's the catch, Jack?"

Jack winces and I wonder if I have learned anything in my whole life about being gracious. "I don't blame you for saying that, Laura. If it's any consolation, I didn't like me much, either. I was too pushy, too unwilling to listen, reluctant to give without some payback. I'm proud to say this right here and right now: I've changed, as much as a man can change in such a short time. Laura, I'd be honoured if you'd agree to have dinner with me next week before I have to go back to the States. Very wonderful things are happening and I'd be grateful for the chance to tell you about them."

"Oh, I don't know, Jack, perhaps we'd best let sleeping dogs lie? I'm quite caught up with the United Way and some other projects. I don't need to—"

"I understand. I promise I'm not asking you to be involved in anything, but I'd like to tell you what I'm doing, no hidden agenda, no scam. I'm not in any pyramid or

Ponzi scheme. I'm not selling, just telling. I'd enjoy your company for dinner while I tell my story. My treat. You still do eat, don't you?"

Jack is the most charming man in two ballrooms. His hair and beard, the crow's feet in his tasteful tan, his respectful concern for my opinion of him, that cologne— what a package! I don't mean romantically. It's not that, never with Jack Beaufort. But one can enjoy being in the company of a charming man, can't one? A man who has evidently encountered good manners and good fortune?

I open my evening bag for one of my calling cards, and hand it to him. "You may call me tomorrow," I say, perhaps a bit more coolly than I wanted it to come out, but I have to say I'm all at sixes and sevens. "I'll check my i-thing to see what's available."

+++

I check my calendar as soon as I get home, of course. I do have a few engagements ahead, though none in the evenings. When Jack calls, however, I'll challenge his first option, no matter when he suggests we meet. Not good to appear too available.

Anyway, I'm still unsure about accepting his invitation at all, once out of range of that cologne and suavity. He's lost a lot of weight, too, maybe too much, but he looks well. Until I saw him at Government House, my feelings about him lay somewhere between unpleasant and nasty. Memories of our encounters had surfaced from time to time since our falling-out but I hadn't allowed them to stay. The best way I knew to be happy was to continue avoiding him.

"Hello, Laura, it's Jack. How are you today?"

"I—I'm fine, Jack, thank you. How are you?"

"Well, you know." He sounds upbeat. "I'm a lot better than I expected to be. I've been seeing a lot of people, and some of it is tough going, but we're getting through it. I'm still alive. I had a great visit with my daughter yesterday."

"That sounds—that must be challenging for you both," I say. What *do* you say?

"Thank you, yes it is. But the outcome will be worth it, for both of us, I think. Now, speaking of enjoyment, have you found an opening for dinner with me?"

Rats. I was expecting Jack to start fully-loaded with a date, not an open calendar. I can't suggest a date and then say I can't make it.

"Oh, right, I forgot," I lie. "Uh, let me check, will you?" I put the phone down, then pick it up and say, "I'll be right back, hang on."

I put it down again and go down the hall to my bathroom. Why? I have no idea. To think, apparently. Where the phone can't see me. I need to get a grip.

Get a grip, I say to the sheepish woman in the mirror. Then I go back to the phone.

"Sorry, Jack, it was in my—uh—my study. Here we are. Let me see now, hmm. My, how things do pile up, even in retirement. How about—no, that won't work—okay, how about Thursday? Thursday evening any good, or no?"

"Oh, not till Thursday?" He sounds disappointed. "Well, that's okaaay. Can we make it an early dinner, say five for six?"

Damn.

"Sure, Jack, five will be fine."

Why wouldn't it be? I'm trying to keep him as he was, even as I sense he has turned a corner that'll make him easier to be around. Dinner shouldn't be too great a sacrifice for me to make. Chalk it up to curiosity.

After all, I've changed, too, without work to keep me edgy. And United Way is all about helping, and we Unit Leaders have attended mandatory workshops to learn how to be nice so we won't give our volunteers reasons to quit. I've been learning to use gentle persuasion instead of demanding obedience. It's tricky, seemed inefficient at first, but I'm getting the hang of it.

On Thursday my intercom rings precisely at five. He's waiting in the lobby, seated on one of the benches by the ferns. He jumps to his feet when I exit the elevator.

"Good evening, Laura. May I say you look lovely this evening."

"Oh, Jack, do try to hold back the blarney." Then, since I am wearing a new outfit and new shoes, I add, "But thank you."

We step outside. The driveway is a very tight turn-around at the front door, just room enough for a car to deliver a passenger and drive off again. Off to one side, three short-term parking spaces are reserved for visitors. I can't see which car is Jack's because the area in front of the door is completely filled with a midnight-blue stretch limo.

"Somebody important must be visiting," I say. "Not un-usual in this building. Or else there's a prom. Are you blocked in?"

"Somebody important indeed," Jack says, and opens the limo's back door, gesturing that I should get in.

"Your—a limo? Are you kidding? What's going on?"

"It's just a taxi, Laura, really. I thought we might as well ride in comfort."

I get in the limo and sink into the soft blue leather seat. Jack gently closes the door, and while he walks around to the other side I am enveloped in the serene surround-sound of some New Age music.

Jack gets in, fastens his seat-belt, and presses a button at his elbow. "Mo, this is Ms Lloyd," he says to the intercom.

"Good evening, Meez Lloyd," says the intercom, and far forward though the smoked glass panel I see the driver touching his cap. "Welcome aboard. At your service, ma'am."

"Thank you," I say. I'm not *un*accustomed to bits of luxury, but I'm not accustomed to being treated with deference in Halifax. Now I know one place to get it.

"Ms Lloyd says 'thank-you', Mo," Jack says. "We're ready to roll."

The car is moving before I notice, partly because the windows are darkly tinted, partly because we seem to be coasting through calm water rather than on potholed streets. I know good suspension, and this vehicle has it.

We're heading along Robie Street toward Bedford Basin. Blue lights glow along the extended side shelves of the car.

"Now, about that cocktail," Jack says. "May I?"

He has crouched to a side seat, picked up a crystal tumbler from its slot and is holding silver tongs over a silver ice bucket.

"On the rocks or neat?"

"What am I having?" I ask.

"Your choice, as long as it's not too exotic. Gin, I think, is your preferred poison?"

"It is indeed. On the rocks, please, would be very nice. Stirred. One twist, since I see you have some."

I say no twice as he points the tongs to olives and Vermouth, and thank you once as he hands me my cocktail.

It's my version of a martini, just as Huston used to cook for me, but served in crystal in the back of a stretch limo while passing by ships at anchor in Bedford Basin. Some days are diamonds.

"Here's to the best of all possible worlds," Jack says, tipping his neat single malt towards me.

"*Slainte*," I respond. When in doubt, speak Gaelic.

I'm enjoying the view. I'm usually behind my own wheel along this busy road and can't risk gawking at sailboats on the choppy blue water, circling the ships at anchor or sailing under the bridge at the Narrows.

"Any clues as to where we're going?" I ask. "Not that it matters. I'd be quite happy to keep this up for the evening, just riding and pretending."

"Pretending. That's a word familiar to me. What are you pretending, Laura, if I may ask?"

"Oh, you know, the usual," I say to the window. "That this is my limo, my driver, that I'm having a top-shelf adult beverage in pleasant company."

What am I saying? I turn toward Jack. "Of course, I don't have to pretend about the cocktail or the company. "

"Thanks, I think," Jack says, laughing. "I can't imagine that I'd be part of your fantasy, but it is nice to be considered pleasant company. I'll do my best to stay there. Top you up? We have a few minutes before our destination."

"Yes, please, I guess. Not knowing our destination, I don't know whether I should sip responsibly or knock it back. I have experience in both."

"Can't guess?" Jack says.

"How would I—oh, Inn on the River? You wanted us to go out there before—before," I finish lamely.

"Exactly. I hope that's okay. The chef is an old buddy and he's promised to impress us tonight."

"You'll never catch me objecting to good food," I say. "This is a night of impressions, Jack, I must say, all of them positive so far."

Both of us advanced our careers by being able to chat amicably with anyone over cocktails, which we do now, though the air inside the limo is filled with question-marks. *Patience, Laura. You've been learning to be in the moment, and this is a pretty good moment.*

We're shown to a corner booth in the Inn's cosy little pub, not the dining room. All the other booths have *Reserved* signs on the table. Two men are sitting at the small bar at the far end of the pub, quietly watching a game on the television. It's not a private room, but we have privacy.

Our wine is poured and it is very, very good. We didn't order it. Jack has left all selections to the chef, and we are willing recipients of his choices. A basket of savoury morsels arrives to keep us thirsty while we resume talking small. I find I don't want to talk small.

"You said you had something to tell me," I say. "If you want. Or not. I'm easy either way."

It doesn't hurt to smooth the way for Jack. Anyway, I'm darn curious.

"Yes. Yes, I do, Laura, thanks for asking. I've been on a most extraordinary journey since I filed for—since I went bankrupt. It might sound dramatic to say that I hit bottom, but I sure was very, very low for quite a while. Aside from the money from our business, which I managed to filch before the account was frozen, I had nothing. So I flew to Florida with some of that money. Have I thanked you for that? I do so now. It made the rest of my story possible, and I will never forget your generosity."

"It wasn't given as graciously as you are thanking me for it now."

"That doesn't matter, Laura, not to this beneficiary. Reluctant charity is still charity to those who need it, and I needed it desperately."

"You're welcome, then. It wasn't just my money, anyway. It was money our business earned. A few thou were immaterial to me, I'm happy to say, but I'm glad it was of use to you. So—you fled to Florida? Good choice. No high heating costs there anyway."

He laughed. "You got that right. It's hot except when it's not, and dry except when it's wet. But there are worse places to be if you happen to be homeless, which I was for a while. "

"My God, Jack—homeless? As in no place to live? I mean, I don't know if I could do that. No, I know I couldn't. Living on the street with people who are spaced out on who knows what—"

"It's true, many are addicts or mentally ill, and I don't just mean the cops." He smiles. "Sorry, gutter humour. Some folks just ran out of all their luck, like me. The recession wiped out many regular working people who had been seduced by easy debt. Many days I slept alongside people who used to be well-employed but now had even less than I had, and I accepted food from charitable organizations and restaurants, bless them. They kept me from having to panhandle, at least. I barely noticed what I was doing or where I was at first, I was so distracted by the battle waging inside my head."

"Poor you." Do I sound empathetic? I mean to.

"Yes, poor me. Anyway, one day I must have been feeling a bit more—uh—sane, settled, maybe, when I noticed some of the workers at a soup kitchen struggling to get their work done because not enough volunteers showed up. Well, I thought, I can ladle soup. So I offered to work all day, set up, clean up, whatever, in return for a meal if there was anything left after I'd served the lineup, and a place to wash up. Eventually someone was desperate for help and said, 'Yeah, okay, whatever,' and I was in. After that, I had experience, see, so I could climb back up the corporate ladder, breadline-style."

Jack smiles ruefully. Neither of us would ever have imagined that the bottom rungs of any ladder of success could start that low.

"Don't tell me you own a profitable chain of soup kitchens now, Jack."

"Hmm, interesting concept, but no, that's not how it went down. It's a pretty fantastic story, though. May I continue telling you?"

The waiter brings new wine and Perrier, and serves our first course, a delicious salad of pear slices, blue cheese, some greens, and walnuts. The pear is like butter. The dressing is ambrosia.

"Yes, of course, please do," I say, distracted by the delicacies on my plate. "You've cleaned up nicely, Jack, if that's not being rude. I'm curious how you made it from a warm Florida gutter to this classy evening with me in chilly Nova Scotia."

"Thanks. How's your salad, by the way?"

"Perfect."

"Mine, too. Life is good, very good," Jack says solemnly, like saying grace before a meal. He consumes his salad quickly, and then continues.

"So, one day, I saw a notice in the place where I was peeling potatoes, inviting volunteers to help open a new church in the suburbs. The notice wasn't meant for us vagrants, of course, it was for church volunteers. But something told me that it might be interesting to go see what there was to see. It's not like I had a lot of other things to do all day. So I cleaned up, shaved, even bought a new shirt and tie at the Goodwill for three dollars—a brand new brand-name shirt, still had the tags—and I showed up at the appointed time and got on the bus just like I was a regular Christian. I knew a couple other passengers from working at the kitchen, and I'd learned to talk the talk. And a tie still makes an impression. My fortunes began to turn around at that moment, though I didn't know it yet."

Our server removes our empty salad plates and returns with piping-hot cups of creamy seafood chowder. It's hard to hear Jack speaking over my inner epicure shouting bravos.

"I just know you're going to get born again in this story, Jack. I'm sure there'll be a book. Will there be testifying? Speaking in tongues?"

"Ah, Laura, that's one of the things I like about you: always speaking your mind. There may be a book someday, but for now you'll have to suffer through my story as I tell it, but no testifying, no tongues. I trust the chowder will keep you in your chair?"

I smile and nod in appreciation. I realize this is the first time I had smiled since Jack met me in the lobby. I must seem like a well-dressed battle-axe.

"Okay, so this was Florida, which means anything goes, church-wise. This new church preached what they call the prosperity gospel, meaning, in short, it's okay to be wealthy. In fact, they say, God chose their members to be wealthy and have stuff, lots of stuff, whatever stuff you want, you just have to 'believe on it'. I'm no biblical scholar, but there's some adroit reading of the Bible in that church."

"It's odd to hear you defending the scriptures, Jack. Got a f'rinstance?"

"Sure. You're familiar with the Twenty-third Psalm, I assume?"

"I am. I believe it comes shortly after Psalm Twenty-one, a personal favourite of late."

"Really? I don't know that one, but I'll look it up." He enters a note in his smart phone. "But everyone's heard 'The Lord's my shepherd, I shall not want'. Well, 'I shall not want' is interpreted by this church to mean that the-Lord-my-shepherd will get me whatever stuff I want. House, car, big TV."

"Yikes. It sounds greedy, don't you think?"

"I *do* think. However, I wasn't there to judge—or believe—but to observe. They do have one point: you can't do much, for yourself or for others, if you don't have at least some wealth. My own definition of wealth was, and still is, anything of value in excess of your basic needs. In Florida I saw great wealth everywhere. Me, I had none and I wanted some. That's nothing new. I always wanted to be wealthy, and was so focused on getting there that I didn't notice I was losing faster than I was gaining. Lesson learned. For the first time in a long time I began listening to voices *outside* my head instead of the ones inside which were not making me wealthy at all. Heck, I was still carefully peeling off twenties from your bankroll, but each twenty had to do me for a week, not an hour, not just for a tip."

"Speaking of that," I say, "where did you keep your greenbacks while you were homeless?"

"On me," Jack says. "My shoes and other places. Safe from pickpockets, for sure."

"Ew. Sorry I asked."

"Sorry I told you. So we volunteers were being interviewed for various tasks for the opening of this church. I thought I'd be folding programs or setting up chairs, maybe get a coffee and some cookies, but it was more like a real job fair, just no salaries offered. The organizers, the people with wealth, were not giving it away if they could help it. Anyway, I made sure I got in the lineup for the tasks I had experience in, like marketing, publicity, promotion, broadcast media and things of that sort. When it was my turn to interview, I closed the line."

"What does that mean, 'closed the line'?"

"I mean that they put me in charge of all those jobs. I beat out a long line of inexperienced, retired, evangelical volunteers, though I selected a couple to do some of the work for me. Pretty good going, eh? I may have had tougher interviews in my life, but none with a more critical outcome. I negotiated a stipend for my duties, too, cash only. The bus ride back to the city was a pretty happy one for me, I assure you. I was able to afford a bed in a scary place where I could finally shower and shave regularly."

"Rags to riches," I say.

"You got that right. When you're just a couple twenties away from zilch, it doesn't take much to change your circumstances, if—and I take full credit for this part—*if* you have the will to make the change. Lots of desperate people can't or won't change whatever keeps them down, but I don't judge them. The weight of society presses very heavy on you when you're at the bottom of it. And you know you're at the bottom when your pillow is made of cement. Or dirt."

"Thank God I haven't had to learn that lesson," I say. "Maybe the-lord-my-shepherd chose me to have stuff, too, but I did all the heavy lifting without noticing any divine help, thank you very much. I may not define wealth as close to the bone as you do, but I am comfortable."

"I'm glad you are, Laura. And let me be clear: the message of this church is not my message. I personally think it's crap."

"Oh. Glad to hear it."

"I'm not against making money, but I just think they're confusing faith with wishin' 'n' hopin', and not in a good way. Mind you, their collection plate is *very* heavy, so they can, and do, make newsworthy contributions to other faith-based charities. It's easy to scorn their getting, but not their giving, though those at the top do live very, very well. You could say that about any of the traditional churches, I suppose. Not evil necessarily, but a necessary evil."

Jack breaks off as our server removes the very empty chowder cups and sweeps crumbs from our linen table-cloth. I'm enjoying everything, I have to admit, even our conversation. It's almost as good as the sizzling steaks that arrive next.

"So then," Jack resumes, "I was working for this church as well as dishing out hash to those now *less* fortunate than myself. My head was spinning. I knew there was a message there for me and I was tuning in desperately to hear it when it came."

"Like those big antennas that listen for signals from outer space."

"I hadn't thought of it that way, Laura, but yes, that's exactly how it was. I was listening for clues that there was an intelligent life for me to live, somewhere in the universe. Meanwhile, I was feeling much, much better in my head than I had for some time, and I didn't mind that I was doing familiar work while I waited for—for my antenna to start beeping. I like that image."

Jack smiles as he carves into his thick and juicy steak. "So the big church finally opened and the place was filled to capacity. All twenty-five hundred seats, can you believe it? They had closed-circuit TV cameras going, broadcasting to the overflow crowd—all praying and singing and giving—in a nearby warehouse. I was interviewing and analyzing feedback response cards like crazy. Does that surprise you?"

I shake my head and roll my eyes, but I smile too. Why rain on this parade?

"It should not go without saying, friend Laura, that I followed your teachings as well as I could recall them, about asking the right questions. I nearly called you then, to get your guidance."

"You knew I wouldn't have answered. Go ahead and eat your dinner, but continue."

"Right. So I'm sampling the customer experience. The Pastor, a very astute businessman with a lot of personal money invested in this venture, he wants to know everything about his congregation's tastes. Do they like the music, which pieces and why? Do they like to pray standing, sitting, hands in the air, sitting on their hands, do they like to greet their neighbours in the pews, all sorts of things like that. I inserted a little question of my own now and then as I was beginning to detect some signals in my antenna, and I wanted to see if I was correct or crazy."

"Or both," I add, ever the supportive conversationalist. "What sort of question?"

"Would you attend this church even if your faith is weak or never materializes'?"

"I beg your pardon? Would I—?"

"No, not you. I asked *them* if their faith—in Jesus, I suppose, though 'faith' rarely gets specified amongst the faithful, they just have it or they don't—if their faith was quote weak unquote, would they like to feel welcome at this church anyway."

"Well done, Jack! In the odd history of the Christian church, you might have asked the oddest question since Martin Luther asked if anyone could lend him a hammer and some tacks. Really. I wouldn't have thought to ask that, but I would know even less what to do with the answers. Where were you going with that?"

"I'll tell you, but how's your steak?"

"Exquisite. I'm savouring every bite, is that okay? How are we for time? Do you have to go?"

"Please take your time. I apologize for my monologue but I will come to the point soon. The chef has dessert in store for us, too. I wanted us to be able to enjoy dinner and not have to rush through it. There is somewhere I must go later, but we're okay for now. I just want to make sure you're happy to stay at the table and not run off when I continue."

I guess my storming out that time had a lasting effect on poor Jack. "I promise not to leave until my plate is cleaned," I say. "I'm a prisoner of my taste buds. Speak on, Jack. Your story is very interesting so far."

"Okay, here goes. The reason I twigged to ask that question arose from our PeepBo venture. Aw, come on now—you promised."

I'm not really going to leave, but I pick up my napkin as though I will. Truthfully, as soon as my feet hear Jack refer to our misadventure, they're itching to walk. But my feet aren't having the steak; I am.

"Okay, so back when you and I took our break, I made that list, remember? I knew I was on to something, but still hadn't figured out what, and you weren't, well, in a frame of mind to consult with me—which I completely understand."

I nodded my agreement.

"Even when we put on that re-enactment for the class reunion, before we all got sloshed, many of our classmates were shaking our hands and thanking us. Remember that? We just thought we were re-doing a silly college thing. But do you recall what many were thanking us for?"

I shrugged to indicate I didn't recall or didn't care.

"They were thanking us for the thought-provoking presentation, Laura," Jack says, very deliberately, looking at me so directly that I felt I should put down my fork. One tender morsel to go.

"Thought-provoking."

"Yes. Your Fairy Godmother speech. I never could get those comments out of my head. Once we got the theatre thing going, feedback was the same, had we—I mean I— had I been smart enough to ask the right question so people could give the answer they wanted to give. It was —you were thought-provoking. Not farcical, or not very. Not really comedic. Your clever re-working of the Bo Peep rhyme as Old and New Testament Bible verses touched on something that people wanted to hear more about. Without the complicating impediment of religion. Or the gobbledygook of philosophy."

Jack leans back in the booth as though he has just proven the Theory of Gravity. We look at each other steadily for a long moment while I try to process what he has told me. Eventually he moves his attention to his half-eaten dinner, and in the time it takes me to finish my final morsel, he consumes the rest of his and places his fork and knife at the four-o'clock position to signal that he has finished. I do the same, and our waiter materializes to remove the debris.

There is a little wine left in my glass, so I pick it up and admire its beautiful colour. We still haven't spoken. It's not unpleasant to be in Jack's presence when he's calm and thoughtful like this, not hyper.

I almost know what Jack is talking about, because I'd thought about it some myself. When I was writing scripts for our performances, I often strayed deeper into the subject of people lost and found than our farcical production called for, but it was interesting to me so that's where I went. I tried to cover it with a punchline, which was not my strong suit, no news to anyone.

However, I've just consumed a gourmet meal, including a satisfying amount of alcohol. Debating matters spiritual or philosophical is not top of mind at this moment. "Go on with your story, Jack. You're off the street, clawing your way back into society by working at a church that wants you to have stuff. How did you get from there to the man I see before me, whose pillow last night was certainly not made of dirt? Not only did you likely sleep between three thousand thread-count sheets—speaking of stuff—but you've changed. A lot. Fill me in on that."

Before Jack can respond, a bear of a man in a chef's black outfit bustles his way to our booth, bearing a tray with three small plates on it. What is on the plates is more art than food.

"Mario!" Jack exclaims, and the men exchange a hearty handshake. "I thought you'd never show. Mario, I'd like you to meet my friend and mentor, Laura Lloyd. Laura, this is Mario, always my friend and sometimes my mother."

"Pleased to meet you, Mario," I say, receiving a gentler handshake from the chef. "You are a Merlin in the kitchen. But what's this about being Jack's mother?"

The men are both enjoying Jack's joke, but Jack is serious as he explains, "Whenever I ran out of money, which was often, back in the day, Mario fed me."

"Like coming home to Momma," Mario says. "Though I didn't always want to do it."

"Another reluctant benefactor," Jack says. "But you did it, and gave me money, too."

"Not exactly." Mario tilts his big head at Jack.

"No, he's right, and I must tell it as it was," says Jack to me. "I stole money from him."

"And what I will tell you," Mario says as he places his huge paw on Jack's shoulder, "is that he has repaid all the money he, ahem, borrowed, ahem, and then some, plus he over-estimated the value of all the meals he had scrounged here for himself and his clients and dubious dates—present company excepted, ma'am—and insisted I accept payment for all of them, against my wishes. And now he's bringing a very classy lady to dinner and allowing me to try out some new recipes on her, how great is that?"

"Very great," I answer. "I hope the classy lady gets tonight's menu because it is beyond fabulous!"

Both men hasten to assure me that the classy lady is me.

"But why I am interrupting you now," Mario says, "is that I have fabricated this wee confection which I would like you to try while I observe, for reasons which may become apparent. Please indulge me."

He serves me and Jack, places his plate at the end of the table and squeezes in next to Jack. His dessert is the same as ours except it has twin bells on top, made of caramelized sugar.

"Shouldn't the classy lady have the fancy one?" Jack teases.

"Ordinarily, yes," says Mario. "But that's why I'm testing it. It might break apart the wrong way and ruin her clothes. I'm creating it for a wedding dinner, see, and this will be the bride's dessert. Please, enjoy."

We apply our spoons to crème caramel in a basket of sugar threads, which has molten chocolate oozing out of it after the first scoop is removed. It is sex in a spoon, but I refrain from coarse comments and settle instead for humming my approval. The sight of the huge chef delicately attacking his bridal showpiece, without mishap, is just more of the evening's entertainment.

"Well, I just came out to meet this fine lady about whom Jack speaks so highly, and to thank my old friend for his generous patronage tonight. I won't interfere in your evening any longer, unless you would like me to make you the bride's version of this dessert, now that I know it won't explode." He aims this at me with a wink.

I decline graciously. After Mario leaves I say to Jack, "A fine friend you have there."

Jack nods emphatically, and I see his eyes are moist. "The best."

Coffee has arrived. Jack glances at his Rolex.

"Now," I say, "you'll have to quickly bring me up to date on your transformation."

"I've taken more time in the preliminaries than I should have, Laura, but I felt you, of all people, would relate to the details of my turnaround. Thanks for listening tolerantly so far."

All his expense and care this evening, and the best I can show Jack is tolerance?

"One day I was at a breakfast cafe—eating well again —with one of my co-volunteers, a smart guy who'd had several careers in business. You might say he wasn't that smart if he ended up working for free alongside me, but as I said, the recession swept up a lot of good and talented people like a tsunami. His business was ruined. But that's his story, and maybe someday you can ask him to tell it."

"Maybe I will. More coffee?" Our waiter had left us with a French press carafe of dark-roast coffee which balanced the exquisite sweetness of the dessert.

"Thanks," Jack says. "So, I'm in the coffee shop with this guy, who is now my friend and business partner, and checking over some notes. He says to me, 'What's that you got there?' And then he hauls out his own little notebook and flips it open and says, 'Want to share and compare?' Turns out we were both using the church as a lab for our own ideas, and I soon found that his interests weren't foreign to mine."

"Was your canny pastor okay with what you were doing?"

"Not really, though it was some time before he found out, and I'm proud to say he found out from us. We wanted to work for his business for as long as we could, though, because his and our recruiting and retention profiles were similar in many respects. Except he wanted to know what worked for his church and we were interested in what didn't work for it, sort of."

"And I'm wondering why you wanted to know that," I say. "I'm still not sure what you're doing. Not theatre, surely."

"Ah, no. But its roots are in our venture. And it's wildly successful, Laura. We've gone viral, as they say. Hence, my near-instant ability to repay my debts now. I still can't get credit here in Canada, of course, as I'm still under the cloud of bankruptcy, though I'm a millionaire on paper. In the US, where banks were notoriously careless about extending credit before the bottom fell out of everything, I can still get credit. Heck, I could even start my own bank there, and I'll soon have the cash to do it. Don't worry," he says in response to my glance, "I'm not nuts. Or greedy. But I have achieved financial wealth, finally. Anyway, my friend and I came to a meeting of the minds. After a couple very busy months, and with the cash of an angel investor, we launched our venture. My friend is the front man, of course, as I didn't have a permit to work in the US. It's all based on trust, but we said if we couldn't get started on trust, we'd have nowhere to go."

"Hmm," I said. "But doing what, Jack? What are you doing to make you so flush?"

Jack glances at his watch again. "Listen, Laura, I'm sorry to have to do this, but I've a plane to catch. I was going to take a cab from here and send you home in the limo, but would you mind coming to the airport in the limo with me and then Mo will take you home? I don't want to drag you all the way out there if you—"

"Oh, for heaven's sake, Jack, of course that's fine. You've got me this far, you can't leave now without giving me the rest of the story. I'll enjoy an extended ride in that limo, anyway. Let's pay the tab and be on our way. I'm happy to make it Dutch treat."

"No tab to pay here, thanks anyway. I paid Mario in advance, and gratuities, too. I don't ask anyone who knew me before to extend credit to me now. By the way, if you can send any business Mario's way, please do. He won't disappoint. Excuse me while I do this."

Jack takes out his phone and taps out a text.

"Done. The limo will be at the door."

As we walk to the hotel entrance, Jack says, "Laura, you seem more, how should I say, more mellow than I recall? Perhaps you've had a life-altering experience of your own?"

"Who wouldn't be mellow, given the evening you've treated me to?" I reply. "I was on guard earlier, you're right. But you always irritated me, Jack, to be frank, so I was expecting more of that. But no irritation this evening, so I lowered my defences. I'll admit, though, that my defences could be rather offensive in the past. Retirement *has* been life-altering, with new interests, pleasant company, that sort of thing. I do feel much more settled now. Thanks for noticing."

Jack confers with our chauffeur before getting in the limo. When we're on the highway toward the airport, he continues. "Okay, now I'll tell you what all that has led to. We've launched an internet-based business with real-time local chapters opening as fast as we can get to them. It's taken off like crazy, like the best of the dot-com booms paired with the immediacy of a flash mob. The social media, if you don't know, are powerful tools for getting the word out worldwide, except in China and other closed countries, but that'll change. We don't have customers, we have members, all over the world, for about the same cost as one music download."

"Excuse me, but how much is that?"

"Sorry. About a dollar. We're ninety-nine cents, actually. Monthly."

"How can you get rich on ninety-nine cents a month?"

"Easy. You can up-sell and re-sell to members you have, but you can't make a penny on people who don't join if your entry fee is too high. If more businesses followed that principle, they'd be solid. Even so, worldwide, ninety-nine cents ranges from dirt cheap to prohibitive."

"Good point. Proceed."

"Our website guides people into membership through a questionnaire similar to the ones used on dating websites, tailored to our purposes, of course. We added a whip-smart social psychologist to our management team early on, and she sorts out personality types and that stuff for us. We're called Quo Vadis. See here."

Jack reaches into his breast pocket and takes out a small plastic disc which he hands me. In the limo's muted light I see a familiar design and an inscription:

?

Questions are universal.
Answers are personal.
Quests are meaningful.
Quo Vadis

When he sees I've read the message, Jack says, "Turn it over."

I do so and I'm looking at myself. It's a little mirror, with a question mark hovering over my head.

"If my high school Latin still works," I say, "*quo vadis'* means 'where are you going?', right? Or 'whither goest thou?'"

"I bow to you, O Wise Laura. I paid good money to find that out," he says. "*Quo Vadis* was also the title of one of those heroic movies popular when we were babies. Peter Ustinov in a short leather skirt persecuting Deborah Kerr in robes and lots of eye makeup. We have no connection with the movie."

"Ha! I might've seen it. Maybe that's why I knew the translation. My parents were fans of those epics like *Exodus* and *Ben-Hur*. At least they're classier than—never mind."

"Right. Our logo is a stylized question mark. Betcha didn't know that the question mark evolved from the word *questio* itself, the first letter 'q' forming the squiggly part and the final 'o' becoming the dot," Jack says with a smile, and I shake my head to admit my ignorance on that subject. "Not to worry. I've become somewhat of an expert on the nature and history of questions lately. This discus is for you, Laura. I invite you to look us up online. Our motto says a lot very simply and succinctly, but there's much more online that I think you will enjoy."

"Thanks, Jack, I'll look it up for sure."

"Good. I'd appreciate your comments on anything you see there, from our Guiding Principles to the merchandise."

"Merchandise? What are you selling, Jack? Hats? T-shirts? These mirrors, of course."

"Mostly coffee and coffee-makers so far. That discus comes with membership."

"Coffee!"

"Yes. Coffee rated very high in all market sampling. D'you see anyone going anywhere these days without a cup in their hand? Asking people to put their lattés down for sixty minutes of church or anything else is asking a large segment of the population to stay away. Old-style churches can't even get their members to stay for a little bit of fellowship after their services any more, let alone make coffee for it, but urn sludge isn't that much of a draw anyway. We do far better than that. We enjoy gourmet coffee during our meetings, and teas, too, made to exacting standards."

"That does surprise me."

"It did me too, but it's true. Our beverages are selling well on three continents and counting. We've created our own brand, and it's a big draw. I'd give you some, but I can't. Only members and their guests can buy the coffee, and only at our gatherings. We make money on the coffee but it's a tool for us, not the main focus."

"I'm sure that'll be in the Successful Business Strategies course you'll be teaching one day soon. But besides coffee, you're just selling air, Jack."

"So it may seem. Oh, and these."

Jack points to a tiny gold pin on his lapel which I hadn't paid attention to before. I lean over to see it: the Quo Vadis logo, a stylized question mark.

"Our members can recognize each other this way, either wearing the lapel pin or as an earring. We sell more earrings than lapel pins, of course, as hardly anyone wears suits these days, and both men and women wear earrings. They are solid gold, and sell very well at a nice markup. We might develop other merch later on, but we don't want to get into too much. Our strength is our Guiding Principles, as you can read on that discus."

"But—questions? Really?"

"Really. We offer a moderated environment for wide-ranging exploration of questions. And a few other bits. A lot of people have difficulty formulating questions, and they find Quo Vadis to be of immense help. As you know, a bad question will lead to a bad conclusion, right? We forbid evangelism or proselytizing of any kind, even about our own organization. You may've noticed that I merely invited you to look us up online, and that's as strong as it will ever get. Never a hard sell from us. We're here, come see us if you like. That's it. If people want to worship a god or a goat, we encourage them to take it to a church or coven of their choosing. That's the point of QV: we help people find the questions that will bring them to the door leading to the beliefs *they* prefer. If I were the head honcho of a church—or a political party, for that matter—I would stipulate that all my members join QV so they'd learn *why* they wanted to be there. Quo Vadis doesn't compete with any set of principles in the world today, organized or disorganized. QV belongs *outside* the door of all beliefs and disbeliefs—all of them—making us potentially bigger than all beliefs and movements combined."

"No one can accuse you of thinking small," I say.

"Not any more." Jack smiles a handsome smile. "I was thinking small in the beginning. Once we got our minds around the universality of this concept, that's when it made sense. The sky truly is the limit."

Jack pointed to the third line on the disc which I still held in my hand.

"We encourage members to develop quests, too. Quests give direction and meaning to what could otherwise be a lot of wool-gathering, if you'll pardon my near-reference to sheep, or 'air', as you say. I got the idea for that from Victor Frankl, a survivor of the death camps of World War Two. He says, 'Those who have a "why" to live, can bear with almost any "how".' His little book has become my constant companion. Quests give members their 'why'. Religions offer hope for the next life, but *now* is when people want help. Politicians have lots of answers, but seldom to the questions their citizens want answered. QV doesn't screen anyone's quest; we may not even know what it is, we just help members achieve whatever is meaningful to them. We don't endorse anything except our own memberships and merchandise."

"Not even 'shelter the homeless' or 'feed the hungry'? I'd expect that to resonate with you."

"Like the United Way, where I accidentally on purpose ran into you last week? Nope. A corporate 'cause' would distract from our focus. Those issues are political and not universally desired, believe it or not, and our market is universal—or planetary, anyway. We haven't beamed our web address to the bacteria on Mars or beyond, not yet."

"Only a matter of time, then?"

"Likely," Jack grins. "We'll invite them, when we can. Speaking of bacteria, we don't expect current politicians to join Quo Vadis, but the next wave of politicians may come *from* QV members, because they'll know the power of asking good questions rather than flailing about for answers which they later abandon. The electorate, which includes our members, will recognize their language and vote for them. That's huge. The world will be a better place very soon after."

"Dream on."

"We do, but it's all the more reason for us to be very careful to keep to our core message and stay neutral on all topics. Anyway, if a member's quest involves charitable work in your community, then you'll find him or her next to you at the United Way or food bank or on either side of the political fence, giving it their best. Our focus is to help people find meaning in their lives through questions and action, regardless of what portal they think they'll pass through in life or death. Period."

"Very intriguing, Jack. Do I assume you've chosen a quest for yourself?"

"You assume correctly."

"May I ask what it is?"

"You may. My quest is to 'pay it backward'."

"Meaning?"

"Meaning that as I've begun to regain strength in my own life—emotional strength as well as financial—I've embarked on a quest to re-connect with as many people from my past as I can, to re-do our encounters and to improve them if required." He sighs. "I'm afraid improvement is required in most that I can think of. My former business partners. My clients. Mom—my real Mom as well as Mario. My ex-wives and other women I used badly. My daughter. You."

"That's quite a list, Jack. I don't need to be on it."

"Oh, the list is much longer than that, but you are definitely on it. In your case, I don't feel that I have so much to repay in money, although I will do that as I said, to the penny, with interest. Framing you in university—who knows how that affected your life? I confessed to doing it but I want to explore if it harmed you, and make amends if I possibly can. But I have a greater debt to you, Laura, the debt of ideas. That may not be something I can repay in kind, but I will honour it. And I offer you a role in Quo Vadis, if you want it. A significant role."

Jack looks over at me. I can see in the muted light that he is sincere.

"Surely you know, Jack," I say, "the last thing I want at this point in my life is a 'significant role' in a business. Especially a viral internet business, whatever that is. Thanks, but no. I appreciate your appreciation, though. It's refreshing, really. That's sufficient recompense for me. I'll watch your venture with interest, but from the sidelines."

"Okay, but the sidelines will soon be right outside your door," Jack grins. "One of our first Canadian chapters will be opening in Halifax very soon. How do you like them apples?"

"Oh, for—seriously? Here? Florida's notorious for wacky ideas, I know, but you've really found traction in our conservative Maritime culture? What next?"

Jack allows this tactless comment to slip away, for which I am grateful. The limo slows for the airport exit, but doesn't proceed toward the airport terminal.

"Where is he taking us?" I ask.

"Hangars. Chartered jet." Jack winks.

"Bravo! I hope all your exes and other beneficiaries of your quest will enjoy your success as much as I've enjoyed sharing this part of it with you tonight," I say.

"Oh, they are and they will. I have much to share. I've been fortunate. One benefit to me of paying it backward is that I am constantly reminded to take care going forward, so that I don't leave such a trail of destruction for myself to repair in the future. Ah, here we are."

As the limo glides to a stop between a hangar and a snappy-looking small jet, I'm confounded by a pang of regret. I feel I'm about to say goodbye to someone I'd rather not part from just yet, and that someone is Jack Beaufort, dammit.

"You don't have to get out, Laura," Jack says. "It's quite windy outside. We don't want to muss your hair. Our driver has instructions to take you wherever you want to go, as long as you're out of this pumpkin before midnight."

He puts his hand on the door handle and then turns to me. "It would mean more than I can say if you would see me when I can get home again, Laura," he says quietly. "I've spent the whole evening talking—which I know is annoying—but I've been eager to tell you, more than anyone else, what your ideas and support have led me to. Now, I'm leaving without hearing about you, and I think there's a lot to hear."

Does Jack feel that regret as well? I just nod. No, there are not tears in my eyes, I'm not going to let that happen, but they are in my throat.

"Here's my card," Jack is saying. "My personal email address is on it. As you may imagine, we get thousands of responses to my blog and our website and Twitter and so on, which our staff deal with, but this is the one that comes right to me personally."

He taps his breast pocket where he keeps his smart-phone. Over his heart. Oh, stop it, Laura, get a grip.

"I hope you'll use it," he says. "I'll reply if you write. Promise."

When I take Jack's card from him his fingers touch mine ever so lightly. Just in lieu of a handshake.

"Thank you, Jack," I say, as sincerely as I have ever said those words. "For this, for everything tonight. I'm—I am impressed. I'm intrigued. I—"

"You're welcome, Laura. Soon, okay? Gotta go."

I watch him get out, gently close the door, and stride toward the jet, pulling the wheeled suitcase the limo driver gives him from the trunk. In spite of the windy night, I get out of the car to watch the noisy little jet taxi toward the runway where heavy planes are thundering in and out. I see Jack settle in his seat and peer out the win-dow. He sees me and waves, and I wave a big one, just like in the movies.

Mo is at my door to help me back in the limo. I could get used to this.

Once we're back on the highway, he advises me over the intercom that Mister Beaufort has stocked the bar with liqueurs he hopes I like, and I am to help myself to them, or to soda, whatever I prefer. I pour a little Sam-buco and sip it as we glide down the highway.

I think and think. Think and think.

At the outskirts of the city, Mo suggests a little tour of the city lights before disembarking, and I accept. We hit all the high spots, literally, traversing both bridges and circumnavigating Citadel Hill before he finally pulls up in the tiny turnaround in front of my condo.

I allow him time to come around to open my door for me. He escorts me to the lobby and hands me a heavy bag.

"What's this?"

"Compliments of the chef," he says.

"My goodness. May I give you something, Mo, for the extra tour? I really enjoyed it."

"No, please, Meez Lloyd. Mister Beaufort paid me very well."

Up in my condo, I open the bag. It contains a bottle of each of the wines which accompanied our dinner, plus a small white cardboard box. Inside is a fourth dessert concoction with a caramelized figure on top.

It's a question mark.

Wagging their tails behind them

"Come on up, Jack," I say cheerily into the intercom, and press the button to open the door for him.

"Hey, will you please pick up these shoes? Company's here," I call over my shoulder, no less warmly.

"Sorry, sorry. Coming, coming."

"Now, please."

"Instantly, immediately," comes the response.

Jack taps at the door just as the shoe-owner is clearing the shoes away, so he opens the door. "Hello, I'm Roger. You must be Jack. Good to meet you, man. Laura's been telling me about your brilliant venture. Gotta run now but we'll meet again soon. Ta-ta to you, Luv."

Roger gives me a quick kiss on the cheek and is gone.

I would pay large money to see that look on Jack's face a second time.

"Who. Was. That?" he manages.

"Roger, evidently," I say.

"Roger Who? What Roger? Come on, Laura, give. Don't keep me in suspense. I'm overseas only a few months and you acquire a studly young live-in that fast? You never mentioned this in your emails. This looks serious. Is it...is it serious?"

Jack is trying valiantly to keep on top of the moment, but he does have a genuine pallor of concern around the eyes. I decide to have mercy on him. "I'm no cougar, Jack,"

I say, laughing. "But I am an aunt, I have discovered. Roger is my nephew. From Wales, home of the Lloyd clan."

"Nephew! Well! Congratulations!" Jack says with obvious relief. "I—I didn't know..."

"Nor did I. I knew Father was of Welsh descent, of course, but to my knowledge he was not in contact with the roots of the family tree over there. However, roots there are. A whole tree, in fact, and Roger is a very charming branch, don't you think?"

"Oh, I'm sure he is. But why didn't you mention any of this in your emails?"

"I did. I told you I went to the British Isles and brought back a wonderful souvenir, remember?"

"I thought you meant a teacup and saucer or a linen tea towel. Not a live man, a live-in man, relative or not."

"Oh, relax, Jack," I laugh. "It's a long story, too complicated to tell in emails. The short version is that my young boarder is an absolute genius in his field of something-something brain science, and is spending a year here in Halifax to study with the genius brain people we apparently have at the hospital and university. My Welsh Lloyds are not wealthy, alas. Somehow they tracked me down to ask if I could help Roger find a place to stay in Halifax while he does his research. I flew over to Wales to meet them and found them to be absolutely lovely people. It's very nice to find a whole village of people who are like me in so many ways."

"Except for the accent," Jack says, regaining his equilibrium. "I didn't think there could be anyone else like you, let alone a whole village of you. Should we worry?"

"Funny guy. Now you know: I'm as common as rain, in Wales, anyway. Roger reminds me so much of my father, it's uncanny. He's more of a second or third cousin a few times removed than a nephew, but I like the title of Aunt and so I've claimed it, though he insists on addressing me as Laura or 'Luv' if anyone's around. I think he gets a kick out of playing my escort, and I certainly don't discourage him. He's charming arm-candy, and I confess when we go out together many eyebrows disappear as completely as yours did."

"Well, what did you think I would think?" Jack asks, perhaps just a bit stronger than usual. "You've always stonewalled any discussion of your personal interests, and then I was afraid you'd gone and taken a mate before I even had a—before I knew. I...I'm just looking out for you, that's all."

What's he saying? Is Jack interested in me, or is he just being brotherly? Not going there, not today. "So, Jack, we're eating in tonight. Hope that's all right."

"You cooked? Pardon my asking, but is it safe?"

"Yes, it's safe, and no pardon granted," I retort with a smile. "Roger and I learned to make this dish together, actually. We've been having a blast, as Roger says. We both had the kitchen skills of college students, meaning not great. I told him he'd be way ahead in the race for the girl of his dreams if he could cook for her. So we started at the high end. We figured nobody'd be able to compare our cooking if we made dishes like Spanish Paella or Coquilles Saint-Jacques. Neither of us could make meatloaf that's fit to eat, but our braising is better than anyone's. Except for Mom's, of course."

"Your mother was a fancy cook?"

"Not my mother, silly. Your friend 'Mom'. Mario."

"You—you're taking classes from Mario?"

"Not classes, exactly, but instruction. We've had him over a few times to show us how. I had contacted him to compliment him on that fabulous dinner at the Inn. I know you paid for it, but he cooked it. You said to send business his way, so Roger and I hired him to give us private cooking lessons. We got on very well. He brings his wife along sometimes, a lovely person. It's fun. He makes us aim high. He says he won't tamper with my scones, but he won't teach us macaroni and cheese, the cheeky bugger."

"What can I say? Who are you and where have you hidden the Laura I used to know?"

"Oh, her," I say. "She's gone away. This Laura is having a ball. Now, let me fix you a drink and then I'll show you my latest project. Here's my bar menu: I'm taking a mixology course at the community college, too, did I tell you? I figured I'd try quality instead of quantity. I can do a pretty good job on these drinks. Even my mistakes taste good."

Jack selects one of the cocktails on my short, hand-lettered menu, and watches with amusement as I fuss with the precise measurements. His drink requires muddling of some herbs for which I use my new-to-me marble mortar and pestle. It may have previously served in a hospital lab but it was a gift from Roger so I didn't ask about its provenance.

"Here's to you, Laura," Jack toasts simply.

"Thanks. I'll drink to me, too."

"Now, as if your new relative and cooking skills weren't enough, you said you had a new project to show me? What is it?"

I lead Jack to my study to show him some of the manuscript. The study is my former master bedroom. Once Roger arrived, we decided that the two smaller rooms would be fine for our bedrooms, and the larger one makes for a comfortable space where we share office equipment.

"Okay. First, I must set the scene. I had gone to the cemetery to visit my parents' graves, and photographed the Bible references on their headstone. I looked them up, and discovered that dear old Mother and Father had kept up one of their constant debates even beyond the grave. Okay, that's just a family thing. But I also found that the graveyard was an interesting place, given the number and variety of people buried there. So I began to take more of my walks there, and each day I photographed some head- stones, focusing not so much on the people as on their in- scriptions. Jack, it's so interesting. I sorted them into gen- erations, age, gender, *et cetera*. The quotations began to take on characteristics according to demographics. At wartimes and the Depression they were all about 'better times in Heaven', and in more prosperous times they ar- gued with death. It's not earth-shattering, but it's inter- esting."

"So it seems, Laura. Any chance you'll do something with your research?"

"If by 'do something' you mean 'publish', yes. I have a publisher bothering me to finish the first section, mean- ing that I have gone and got myself in a trap of deadlines again. But it's my trap and I really am enjoying it. I'm working with a great photographer, too."

"You? Collaborating?"

"Watch it, smarty, or I'll pour your drink down the sink. Actually, there may be other books to follow. A series, perhaps, to feature the old cemetery near the Pub- lic Gardens, for instance, then the one on Barrington Street, and so on. And there are some markers with non- Biblical inscriptions, too, so we'll see if I have the brains to tackle those."

We return to the kitchen so I can stir the sauce. Jack sets the table while bringing me up to date on Quo Vadis, especially the phenomenal response to his recent trip to Asia. I never wavered about signing on in any official corporate capacity, not because I don't trust Jack—that's long gone—but because I'm enjoying my life now and am very watchful not to go down any roads that might disturb my equilibrium. Working for QV would earn me lots of money, but I have plenty of that for my ambitions, plus enough to support my nephew in his medical research.

I think of it as paying it sideways.

Roger is great company, I must say, overlooking my issues with his size thirteen shoes. He's a smart young man. I like to think it's a family trait. He pays me the ultimate compliment occasionally by asking my advice on some aspect of methodology for his brain research. Even his mentor at the hospital has discussed his work with me when he's been to dinner. I do my best to ask good questions.

Anyway, I'm happy to provide decision support for Jack when he comes to Halifax. I give it my best and I'm well rewarded.

Jack has remained a changed man, though for a long time I watched for signs that the former fast-talking advertising salesman would resurface. That hasn't happened.

I've changed, too. I would like to think it's because I found my true quest on my own, but I will admit that attendance at the local Quo Vadis chapter hasn't hurt.

The Church of Little Bo Peep and other stories

Jan Fancy Hull

Ten Questions

Albert MacLean awoke from an unexpected sleep and feared he had gone blind. He couldn't see anything, so he assumed he had gone blind while he slept. Or maybe it was night. Whichever, he blinked his wide-open eyes to see.

"Shit," he said, and heard his voice echo in the room. He heard no other sound except the whisk of the sleeves of his nylon windbreaker as he struggled to sit upright on a very uncomfortable seat.

As he moved, his feet fell to the floor with two thumps and a strange pain shot through his legs.

"Ow! Ow! Shit!" he said with considerable feeling. His feet had been propped against a wall and his whole lower body had gone to sleep. Nothing was asleep now, as pins and needles invaded all his lower parts from his neck to his bum to his toes, and on top, his head was pounding.

Flailing around in his blindness, Albert MacLean discovered that he could easily reach the walls on both sides of the room he was in. As sensation returned to his posterior, he became aware that there was a large hole in the seat of the chair he was on.

He was in a toilet stall.

"Ow!" he said as he struck his elbow on the edge of what must be the toilet-paper dispenser. "Frig!"

Albert was puzzled. This may not have been the first time he had fallen asleep in a toilet stall, but it was definitely the first time he had been left there until after closing time. Usually a janitor or night watchman discovered him during rounds and chased him out with loud talking, sometimes also shaking a mop or a long-handled flashlight at him.

Once his legs were able to support his weight, Albert stood and opened the door to the stall. He expected some dim light to show him the exit, but he was still unable to see anything at all. Slowly and awkwardly, but without incident, he made his way on wobbly legs to the washbasin counter.

Now, which way to the door? The exit is either left or right, depending on which row of cubicles you chose, but where's the EXIT light, dammit?

He thought of making a complaint to the management of this place about this breach of safety protocol, then decided to never mind. He was unsure of where he was just at this moment, but he was very sure management wouldn't like him being where he was and would not receive his complaint in the proper spirit.

Keeping one hand on the basin counter, Albert tried going left. The end wall arrived, as did a large metal wastebasket, which made a very loud bang in the otherwise silent room when he knocked it against the tile wall.

"Yikes!" he said.

He continued his exploration of that wall but when he arrived at the urinals he recoiled in disgust. He was exploring this washroom with his bare hands, after all.

Working now to the right, he passed the basins again, a paper dispenser, another wall, and then the steel handle of the men's-room door.

Albert pulled the door open and almost wished he hadn't. He sure didn't like being in the stone cold dark, and was glad to discover he had not gone blind, but he was not sure he liked what he saw or heard now—or didn't see or hear, more to the point.

The Muzak was not playing, for one thing. Albert liked Muzak. It was part of what made the mall attractive for him. It was always jaunty and upbeat, and they started Christmas songs even before the radio stations did, though that was a good month away yet. It was still summer.

Albert stepped out into the service corridor. It was illuminated by very dim light emanating from the mall's centre court area. He looked down the long stretch past the stores, past the centre court and the big department store, to where he knew the busy liquor store anchored the other end. Not a freaking soul in sight. Every store closed, each sliding glass door slid shut, no lights inside.

The puzzle forming dimly in Albert MacLean's mind was this: it couldn't be night, because all the lights were off and he could still see, now that he wasn't in the men's. Also, it couldn't be dark outside, because if it was, the million-watt lights they had out there in the parking lot would be glaring into the mall brighter than day, not this grey light.

Albert looked behind him to check that the corridor to the dark washroom was still visible, and it was. It hadn't been much of a home, but in this moment he thought of it as a refuge. If it came to that.

No one could accuse Albert MacLean of being curious. Curiosity often called for bravery, often without warning, so it was his policy not to be curious. But Albert was curious now to learn what was the source of the odd light that brought dimness to the ends of the hallways.

He made his way toward the centre court, slowly, due to residual stiffness from his slumber in the stall, where, he remembered, he had propped his feet against the wall so a cursory inspection by a hasty janitor would not reveal his presence.

As he shuffled he became aware of another odd stimulus: sound.

Albert had not been treating himself all that well of late, or maybe too well. Whichever it was seemed to depend on who you were, and Albert had to be himself. The combination of analgesics he administered to himself sometimes made him less sharp than he might otherwise have been, kept him one remove from bright, shiny reality, like a protective coating over his nerves. Like wrapping a delicate rose in burlap against the harsh winter wind, as he liked to think of it.

Nothing wrong with that. Life was better, he found, when there was not too much of it. While the glitter and cacophony of a shopping mall might seem an odd refuge for one who wanted to deaden the senses, once Albert had acquired his "full metal jacket", as he thought of it, the mall seemed pretty, the piped-in music sounded delightful, the announcements to shoppers were messages to him from one who cared, the workers seemed like family and the regular shoppers like friends, and all of that felt better than the life of Albert MacLean that existed outside this place and outside his numbing drugs.

This new mall experience without the lights and without the noise was disorienting. The odd sound of which he was becoming aware was not Muzak, not announcements, not shopper noises, but a dull, wide, urgent sort of sound, a sound that seemed to be paired with the grey light.

Some lights are paired with sounds, as Albert well knew. Ambulance sirens and revolving red lights, for instance.

Albert slowly approached the food court at the entrance to the Bedford River Mall. He would never have done what he did next had there been people watching, but there didn't seem to be any around. So he flattened his back against the wall as he had seen done on TV shows, and leaned out to reconnoitre around the corner. That didn't work, as Albert's neck was quite stiff and he couldn't turn his aching head far enough to see anything except what was in front of him. He flipped around, belly to the wall, and then allowed himself to peek at the source of light and sound.

"Ho-*ly!*" he said.

Had he seen the Rapture he wouldn't have been any more gob-smacked than at this moment.

The three-storey-high windows were inundated with a wide and steady fire-hose stream of water. That was the first thing he noticed, the water running down the glass and never letting up. The light that struggled through the layers of water and plate glass was mottled and uncertain. It seemed as though the flow would wash away the light. Or the glass itself. Albert had the sensation of being completely submerged *and* in a car wash.

The water hitting the glass, that's what he had heard. Not a nice pit-a-pat rainy-day sound at all, but a nasty, dangerous crackling, like hail, like gravel shot from a car's continuously spinning tires. This wasn't rain. Rain falls down in drops. This was whole water. This was Biblical.

The usual array of twinkling, blinking, revolving, and flashing lights was gone from the mall. Not even any lights on the Spaceship in the food court. Albert loved to watch parents and grandparents resentfully dropping little kids into its cockpit while they enjoyed food court delicacies. Albert loved the tinny boom from the Spaceship's tiny speakers, the flash of lights as the Spaceship launched itself in a slow roll, the squeals (or screams) from the tiny tots. He felt he was one of the family, if only for that moment.

"Holy-moley," Albert said, for all the reasons that confronted him. Where were those over-indulging people now, and the servers who fried their fries?

Above and behind the roar of the waterfall, a very loud roar now that Albert was in front of the expanse of glass, was a siren sound. Albert had never heard anything like it, but he knew it was wind. Screaming wind.

"What the hell?" he whispered.

Albert moved farther into the centre court with no particular destination in mind, but it was instinctive to try a new perspective that would make things look right again. He wasn't going to even try the big, glass double doors against which so much water was being driven. He wasn't going to go through those doors into that weather, no way. Anyway, he knew rightly enough that they were locked, otherwise that wind would fling them wide open like a hyperactive Walmart greeter.

An orange pylon slammed into the glass nearest Albert. He jumped back in fright, slipped, and fell. That's when he noticed that the wide terrazzo-tile floor was covered in water.

"Oh, fer cryin' out loud! Shit! Shit! Shit! Now look! Dammit!"

He was soaked all down his right side from his elbow to his pants and, he saw as he got himself up again, his sneakers.

Albert MacLean was not an especially fastidious fellow. But there was a line below which he tried not to sink in his present state of insulation from clarity, and being soaking wet and falling-down clumsy in public was below that line.

Albert was so accustomed to crowds here in the centre court that he was finding it difficult to keep in mind that he was alone. There really was nobody to see his sneakers filling up with the water draining from his pants, or his shoelaces afloat.

He looked around just to be sure of the nobodyness. All he saw in the flat wavy light was a pool of water, spreading not all that slowly from the front doors, where he noticed it spraying in through the gaps. The flood was heading across the court toward the locked doors and brand-new carpet of the big department store.

"Holy," Albert said again. After a moment's reflection the imminent implication of this situation dawned on him and he said, "Better look out, ya dweeb!"

The big department store's manager was a wiener who had given his security staff strict orders to keep Albert MacLean from setting one toe on that carpet. Albert had never misbehaved in the store, had taken nothing of any value from it, had even sometimes straightened up the mess on the shelves since the little pinch-faced bastard wouldn't hire enough staff to look after the store. But one day the little shit had loudly called Albert a vagrant and booted him out.

Albert's friends at the coffee shop in the food court saw and heard, and Albert was ashamed, but they called him over and gave him a large double-double on the house and kept checking on him until he had calmed down.

He was no vagrant. Albert's inheritance meant never having to say he was sorry. Well, no, it meant never having to ask for handouts; he was sorry about a lot of things that his inheritance couldn't help him with. He had been and said sorry a lot before he found those pills.

"Keep that water off your fancy carpet, why dontcha, you little piss-ant!" Albert said to the locked glass doors, to his own moderated amusement. It was funny, but not that funny right now, standing as he was in inch-deep water, alone, in the middle of the Bedford River Mall centre court.

Along with his head, Albert's back was aching, really hurting. He knew he had aggravated his injury when he fell. This would not be good.

His back was the reason he was in this mess. Not this abandoned, water-logged, un-powered shopping centre mess, but the mess of his life. He once had a decent job, Albert had, working in an office performing a middling function between lesser and greater functions, but he had become injured when wrestling with a tippy, over-loaded, lateral filing cabinet.

Before the accident, Albert's productivity had suffered because of this dangerous filing cabinet and other safety violations in the office. He couldn't help watching in alarm whenever anyone opened the top cabinet drawer, which was frequently. He mentioned the risk to his boss several times, and his boss offered to move Albert's cubicle to where Albert wouldn't have to see the cabinet. He didn't exactly say where.

One day Albert was on the floor, trying to stabilize the cabinet himself, when someone came along and quickly opened the top drawer. All the way. Down it all came on Albert's back.

Spilled files were retrieved and re-filed in a new cabinet and no blood was shed, though Albert did sustain a carpet-burn on his forehead which stung for several days. But Albert's back pain began and worsened from then on, because of the way the loaded cabinet had landed on him.

They fired him for violating company safety rules. His claim for Worker's Compensation was filed, denied, appealed, denied and eventually abandoned. He was worn out, discouraged, and had lost whatever it is that going to work every day means. But he had his inheritance to live on.

Albert's marriage, too, had been unstable and it, too, soon toppled, with collateral damage that lasted longer and wounded deeper than carpet burns. These physical and emotional hurts arose from different injuries but they gave deep pain to the same unprepared man. The pills which made Albert's pains tolerable but not numb, those pills hung on to Albert and would not go away, so he rewarded their faithfulness in kind. If one was good, two were sweet. He became so tired of misery that he kept it at bay pre-emptively. The full metal jacket.

Speaking of which, Albert fished in his pocket for some fresh pills, long overdue, and brought out only fingers-full of wet Kleenex mush. His accidental swim in the flooded court had soaked his pocket and now he remembered: he had accidentally taken two pills together that morning, which made him dizzy. He had gone for the moderate privacy accorded him in the Men's, and promptly passed out in the cubicle with his feet up the wall.

Now he was out of meds. That explained the thumping headache and growing all-over body ache. The curse of those little darling pills was that they'd leave you worse than they found you if you stopped loving them.

He would just have to suffer. Surely someone would open the big doors soon so he could go home where there were plenty of clean, dry pills.

His vision of his warm and dry home received a correction from an extra-strong deluge of wind-driven rain outside. He never paid attention to weather forecasts, had not known a hurricane was coming, and was AWOL in the Men's when the mall had closed before noon. He still assumed that this was just a very, very, *very* rainy day. But one on which he was locked alone in the mall. So, maybe worse than that.

Albert wasn't sure, but he thought this might be an emergency. He should call 911 and report it.

Maybe not. Albert didn't carry a cell-phone. Nobody to call, nobody he wanted to call him. When did they remove public payphones from the world? He couldn't remember if there was one in this mall or in the grocery store across the parking lot or anywhere. Maybe there was one outside the Administration Offices, upstairs on the mezzanine floor alongside a dentist's office and a hearing clinic. He had never been up there, no thanks. No need to attract mall management's attention.

Albert now began to wade toward the curving metal staircase, taking great care not to slip and fall again. The water was getting deeper, no question about it.

Then the storm outside stopped, just like that. In a matter of minutes, the flowing water turned into heavy raindrops, then nothing. The wind's moaning was more audible for a moment without the drumming of rain to cover it, but then it dropped too, and the light from outside was much brighter.

This turn of events did not bring cheer to Albert MacLean's heart, not at all. Before, Albert couldn't see through the windows because of the deluge of water flowing over them. Now they offered Albert a spotty view of the scene outside.

As far as he could see, all was under water. Just this morning there had been a reasonable-sized asphalt parking lot, with concrete curbs and soaring poles with sodium lights on top. Beyond that was a sleepy little river, hence the name of the mall. Beyond that, the street, then another shopping mall on the other side.

All was very wet now and not a living soul in sight. The sleepy little river was bucking and tossing far beyond its banks.

A car backed out of its parking space and turned to drive away.

"Hey!" Albert shouted, and rushed—carefully—to pound on the windows with his palms. "Hey-hey-hey! In here!"

Then Albert realized with a spooky feeling that the car wasn't being driven, not by people. It was floating in the river currents swilling about, rotating lazily.

The Bedford River Mall was built on a small flood plain across which the little river flowed, quietly most of the time, through the usual obstacles of shopping carts and coffee cups, to its nearby outfall in Bedford Basin and out through the Harbour to the sea. As far as Albert could see to his right, to seaward, there was water covering the ground surrounding all the buildings, and only as the road rose up a hill did he see dry land emerge to his left. The water also covered much of the parking lot across the street, and had likely already entered the stand-alone bank closer to the street.

What made his hair stand up was that the drifting car seemed to be drifting up-river. That would mean it was being pushed by salt water. From the ocean. This far inland.

"Unbe-effing-lievable!" Albert said, quietly, as it was much quieter now and he didn't have to shout to hear his commentary. With his medicated fog dissipating, things were becoming somewhat clearer, and somewhat more confusing.

In that clarity, Albert heard water splashing and he knew that somewhere the mall's roof was leaking. No wonder. The height of the barrier around the edge of the flat roof would be the depth of water on it, and that would be heavy. Drains could be overwhelmed, especially if debris was blocking them, and with this wind everything outdoors that wasn't nailed down, and some things that were, would be debris. Fear of the ocean coming in to drown him wasn't enough; he would have to fear the roof falling on him also.

Albert assessed his situation as well as his poor head would allow. He could take refuge from roof collapse under the curving metal staircase to the second level, but he'd be standing in water there, which might rise to his waist or worse. Or he could go up to the mezzanine level, see what he could see up there, and decide then. He wasn't keen on climbing the stairs. Bad backs and fourteen-foot staircases do not get along. But there might be a chair, or he could sit on the top step, hard as that would be. At least the floor would be dry up there, and if he stayed near the outer wall he might be spared if the roof collapsed.

He had dropped that 911 call idea. The apocalypse was happening outside. He'd rather fend for himself in the mall than have a helicopter or a Coast Guard ship pull up.

The empty curve under the staircase was where they sometimes permitted a charity booth or other so-called community support to set up. Dead space used to generate PR for the Mall, is what it was. The twenty-foot Christie the Christmas Tree, another favourite of Albert's, would soon stand there.

An old-style photo booth had appeared in that space recently, but Albert hadn't yet learned its purpose. It wasn't for taking four-for-a-quarter photos, that he knew. Some young people had been working at it for several days. Albert stayed away from any group while they were setting up their display as they were usually stressed at that phase, especially when they discovered that they had no access to electricity there and safety regulations prohibited an extension cord, except when the aforementioned Tree needed it. Once they were set up and the volunteers found that next to nobody visited their dead zone display, they were more open to a visit from Albert.

As Albert passed the booth now and reached the railing to begin his climb, a pleasant female voice from inside the booth said: "Hello. May I please ask you one personal question?"

The sound Albert made in response to this sudden greeting was vocal but without consonants or vowels, not a very manly sound but one very much of surprise. He might have slipped and fallen again had he not been holding the railing, but his violent lurch again triggered more pain in his back, which he was just frightened enough to overlook.

Albert stared slack-jawed at the booth. The brown curtain was pulled across the opening, but it covered only the upper half and below it in the booth he did not see any legs that could belong to that voice. No legs at all.

"Wh-what?" he ventured softly. "Buh-beg pardon?"

When responding to a possible hallucination, best policy is to be polite.

There was no response.

Albert's mind was racing, going nowhere fast. He began to perspire. "Hello?" He cleared his throat and tried again, a little louder. "Hello, who, um, who's there?"

No answer. Albert tried to release his hand from the railing but he had gripped it so tightly that he needed his other hand to pry his fingers loose.

He took a hesitant step toward the booth and the voice spoke again, so very pleasantly. "Hello. May I please ask you a personal question?"

"C-come out here and ask it then," Albert replied with mounting fright just one second before realizing that he was talking to a recording. He was yet again grateful nobody was there to see him.

Slowly, still wary, he reached out to draw the curtain open.

Empty.

He leaned his head inside. A light came on overhead and the Voice said, "Hello, my name is Jenna Beaufort, I'm a sociology student at Saint Vincent's University. I'm creating a profile of Bedford's collective personality and I need your assistance. This will take only one minute and is entirely confidential and private. Please be seated."

Fascinated to find these comforting sounds and lights in the midst of the disaster in the mall, Albert sat.

"Thank you. Now, I will ask you a question and you will have sixty seconds to record your answer. There are no right or wrong answers. What comes right off the top of

152

your head is what I want. When you are ready, please press the red ASK button in front of you."

She sounded so nice. She reminded Albert of the woman in the mall Administration Office who made announcements such as, "Attention Shoppers, the Mall will be closing in ten minutes. Please complete your purchases now. Thank you for shopping at the Bedford River Mall and please come back again soon." Albert often stayed at the mall until he heard her. Sometimes she added "Good night," which he liked a lot.

But this booth girl—Jenna, did she say?—was something else. She was young, she seemed eager, educated, warm, a person in need of his assistance and asking him for it respectfully. And she said there are no right or wrong answers. She was lying, of course, or maybe just naive, as there are always wrong answers, Albert MacLean knew that as well as anybody and better than some. But still, she was making him an intriguing and rare offer: to sit down and answer her question.

A thought wiggled through Albert's uncombed mind that this young lady might actually be listening live, on the line, sitting warm and dry somewhere, not aware of how stormy it was with him at this particular place and time.

"Hello? Wh-where are you calling from?" he asked the booth. "We're having a pretty bad storm here. I'd like to report some s-serious flooding. The power's out. Bedford, Nova Scotia. A man is locked in the big mall there. Here."

Nobody was on the line.

He reached out to push the red ASK button on the wall opposite him in the little booth. When it had been an actual photo booth, the camera would have been behind a glass which also served as a mirror for the posers. The mirror effect was still there in the yellow overhead light, and Albert saw himself in the glass, darkly. It was not a pretty sight. It could be said that a tossed haircut is stylish, a scruffy beard is sexy, or rumpled clothes are street casual. Albert couldn't muster any such descriptors about his appearance. He looked like a bum, the way he always hoped he didn't look. And sad. A sad clown of a bum.

Albert couldn't prevent the tears that annoyed his eyes. Frustrated, he hit the red ASK button.

"Thank you," said Booth Girl's lovely voice. "You will have sixty seconds in which to record your response. Please speak clearly, but there is no need to shout. Here is your question: What is your favourite virtue? What is your favourite virtue?"

Albert heard a click and knew a device would record every word if he uttered any. He wanted to play her game, but what kind of question was that? His favourite what? Who ever talked about virtue, especially in a hurricane? What is a virtue, anyway?

He noticed a little clock illuminated behind the glass screen, the second hand sweeping from 60 down toward zero. He had fewer than twenty seconds left. A virtue?

"Chastity!" he shouted, just before the hand reached zero.

"Thank you very much for your help," the voice said, with great sincerity. "Have a nice day."

"Spank you very much for your help," Albert MacLean said rudely. "Have a shitty day."

He got up from the stool in the booth with great difficulty due to the pain radiating from his lumbar region to his legs, and re-entered the wet and lonely Bedford River Mall.

Albert ascended the staircase one step at a time, bringing up his very bad leg and steadying himself on each step before stepping up again with his not very good leg.

He hadn't allowed his full metal jacket to wear off like this in a long time and he was dismayed by the power of the pain he was having. In a sort of reverse remorse, Albert realized that he really had been injured by the filing cabinet and really did need pain medication, and here he'd been beating himself up for being just a spineless wimp with a needless drug habit.

"Definitely not spineless," he said through gritted teeth. "I wish."

Albert would ask to come back as a spineless jellyfish if he had to be reincarnated, but first he would ask for a free pass. One life was more than enough for Albert. Earth's gravity was far too strong.

It was on someone else's recommendation that Albert had begun taking these extra-extra strength, over the counter pain pills after his doc had declined to prescribe stronger ones. It was supposed to be just until the Worker's Comp circus was over, the theory being that his demonstrated need for codeine would strengthen his claim. That someone else had been Albert's feckless lawyer.

Remembering this always led Albert to another murky memory he preferred to avoid: that the gormless weasel lawyer handled his divorce, too. He seemed very appreciative of the about-to-be-ex Mrs Albert MacLean's point of view, and possibly of her other attributes as well.

There were man-eating pythons lurking along that memory-path and Albert usually drove them back with his pharmaceutical armaments. Because a medical professional was not monitoring Albert's use of these drugs, there was nobody to warn him that they could be ineffective but addictive.

At the top of the staircase, damp with sweat from his fright and his pains, Albert was relieved to spy a padded vinyl waiting-area bench on the landing outside the Administration Office. It looked like a bed in a luxury hotel to Albert at this moment.

About this time, the storm returned. The volumes of water and wind were just as they had been before.

Albert viewed the show from his balcony. He was closer to the windows and to the roof than he had been before and their noises were unpleasantly amplified by this proximity. He surveyed the open court below, and saw the apron of water beginning to creep forward again.

He saw it and he didn't care. It was down there and he was up here. What he cared about was that beautiful, armless, cushioned bench, waiting just for him in front of the Administration Office. He walked with his arms reaching out as toward an embrace. He knelt with first one knee and then the other on the bench, and slowly lowered himself down sideways, facing inward, his back to the world so he would hear and see the least.

Arms wrapped around himself, soaked side up, Albert MacLean dropped immediately into a deep and drugless sleep.

+++

A voice woke him.

Albert had no idea how long he had slept. Sure, he wore a watch, a very nice one, too, but he was not in the habit of referring to it for information such as the time of day or date of the month, as he hadn't found those details relevant for some time. It also glowed green if he pushed a button but he had forgotten about that feature.

However long it had been, there was still daylight of a sort coming in the big windows, though it was much reduced from before, so he assumed it was nearing sundown. Sundown? The sun was nowhere near the Bedford River Mall today. The world may have spun out of its orbit to go flying toward deep space, for all he knew.

Then he remembered why he woke: he had heard voices. Hallucination? Nightmare? They weren't unusual.

"Hello?" he called into the back of the bench. "Up here! Help! Hey!"

Albert heaved himself upright with difficulty. One arm was asleep because he had been lying on it. His headache was very loud.

He made his way to the railing, shaking out his arm as he went to bring back circulation, and called again, "Hello! There's somebody up here, hello?"

More water had leaked into the court below, enough that the whole area was submerged. By golly, it must have soaked far inside the jumped-up little knob's big store by now, Albert saw, but he didn't pause to enjoy that spectacle at the moment.

"Hey!"

He leaned over the rail, noting that it was dangerously low and a person could fall if he wasn't careful. He also noted that the photo booth had a visitor: a plastic wastecan from the food court. It hadn't been there earlier. It was right in front of the curtained entrance to the booth and Albert would've had to go around it to get in and out of the booth, and he hadn't.

Who moved it there?

As Robinson Crusoe discovered before him, evidence of another human on your deserted island elicits both joy at the potential of a companion, and fear at the potential of an enemy. Mostly it was fear that filled Albert's beleaguered breast. What sort of Man Friday had come into Albert's mall?

The waste-can began a slow spin away from the booth. "Hello," the booth said cheerily to the floating can, "may I ask you one personal question?"

Both joy and fear may be superior to disappointment.

Albert was in a bad way. He was hungry and thirsty and he had to pee. His head was pounding, his joints were aching. His back was—by golly, his back was *not* aching, not like before. Oh my goodness, Albert had just got up from the bench and walked over to the rail like he was normal. The torture-demons were not pressing on his sciatic nerve, at this particular moment at least.

Maybe his fall had knocked something back into place. Can that happen? Maybe that unyielding bench had just the right therapeutic effect on his injury. Whatever the cause, Albert at this moment was back-pain-free and drug-free. His headache, he thought, might also be the effect of being drug-free and might go away on its own, sometime. It would have to for now, as he had no little white goodies with him. There were lots in the mall's pharmacy, he was certain, but he wasn't about to resort to smash-and-grab yet, though maybe later he would, for food.

Food. That very waste-can down there often received a shameful amount of perfectly good food. He couldn't count the times he had sat in the food court and watched one customer after another toss out most of their biggie-sized order, while at another table some desperate soul sat counting coins to see if they could buy something that was too costly and no good for them anyway.

Albert never intervened, that was his strict policy. An unsolicited approach from Albert, regardless of his intent, was rarely well-received, so he remained a passive, though not disinterested, observer.

Only one time had Albert ever broken that policy. A man had been making frequent visits to the mall, trying to be invisible. Sort of like Albert, but with sinister intention. Well, hey, that's what mall cops are there for, isn't it, to see the invisible people? This guy was good, often coming in or going out ahead or behind shoppers, holding the door for them, smiling, chatting, making it look like he was with them.

This one day, a too-young mother of several babies, a regular, was herding her littles through the food court mayhem when one of her drooling brood had wandered away from her distracted attention toward the lure of the Spaceship. Mister Invisible watched for his moment and then strode toward the child like a wolf cutting a stray lamb from the herd, smiled and waved at the mother, who wasn't looking at him, said just loud enough so she wouldn't hear him that he'd take the child out to change its diaper, and he opened his arms to scoop the child but found Albert MacLean had materialized in his embrace instead.

Albert had stood his ground, nose to nose with the would-be kidnapper, dead-eye to eye. Mister Invisible hastily left the mall and never came back. Albert shooed poopy-pants back toward his family, and didn't look up to receive the mother's suspicious glare. Then he went back to his table and trembled so hard for so long that his coffee was cold before he could safely lift it.

Other than that, Albert had not intervened in the human dramas that played out in the Bedford River Mall every ding-dong day. He still felt fright when he thought of that near-abduction and the many ways that it could have gone all wrong for Albert MacLean. But he wasn't about to let it go wrong for that baby or its unaware child-bride mother, not if he could help it, not that day nor any day.

Back to the waste can, a proper name for this object if there ever was one.

The mall was open as usual yesterday morning, he calculated, and had done a slow business ahead of the storm, when Albert had gone into the washroom for his little snooze, during which the present hell had been unleashed. No, not yesterday morning. Today morning. *This* morning. His deep sleep on the bench and ripping headache had disoriented him more than was the norm, and who could blame him?

That wasn't the issue. The issue was that there was likely something edible inside that waste can. Albert needed no more incentive to descend the stairs, still moving very, very carefully, and step into the ankle-deep water.

Scrounging for food was a field in which Albert was a novice. Another first for him, a new low. Had there been people around, Albert would have starved rather than be seen bin-diving, would have starved right to dust. But he didn't see the necessity of dying just yet. That might be a later consideration. Right now, he was very hungry and thirsty, signs of being very much alive. The pills may have dulled those sensations hitherto, but now his stomach was loudly and clearly demanding to be fed just like the children in the food court.

There was a slight current in the water, Albert saw, moving in the front doors and moving down the corridor towards the liquor store. He was glad that the water was running out somewhere. He had a fleeting vision of the whole mall filling up to the top like a huge aquarium, he its only fish.

He reached the waste-can. Jenna in the booth said, "Hello. May I please ask you one personal question?"

"Later, babe," Albert said. "Got work to do."

The can wanted to play tag, but Albert trapped it against the steps and wrestled off the top. Not a lot of *garbage*-garbage in there, he was happy to see, which is why it was light enough to float in this shallow pond, and nothing looked too grotty in the fresh, black liner bag. As luck would have it, a discarded coffee had landed sippy-side up in the bag-lined can. Careful of his back, he reached in and retrieved the cup.

"Bingo!" Albert crowed. "Jackpot!"

It was the remains of his very own coffee which he had carefully discarded that very morning on his way to the washroom. He knew it was his because the outer layer of the paper cup was shredded in his unique way, an un-thinking habit as he sat, peeling down the sides. It was a miracle that the lid had stayed on, that the cup had kept its contents.

He put the half-full cup carefully on the stairs as though it was hundred-year-old scotch. A quick swish around the other contents in the can brought up a frosted, doughy, cinnamon swirl in a styro container with only one small bite missing from the bun. A child-size bite.

Albert remembered seeing that child, remembered wondering what the grandparents expected the babe to do with such a thing. "Milk!" he had wanted to say to them. "Give that child milk! And fruit! And hugs!" But that was not his policy.

Jenna once again entreated Albert to visit, and turned her heart-light on to welcome him, so he took his glean-ings into her curtained boudoir, sat on the stool and enjoyed his feast, fastidiously using retrieved napkins to cover his dirty fingers.

Once his dinner was consumed and the reduced refuse recycled back to the floating receptacle, Albert really needed to pee. Wading all the way back down the dark hallway to the Men's seemed fruitless, since there would be no running water and no lights in there, and the odds in favour of getting his stream in a urinal and not on his soaked shoes in the pitch blackness were not great, though maybe that point was moot. Could be the sewer was backed up and dribbling out of the bowls anyway. That would be a delight to have flowing down the corridor. Something to look forward to.

Albert's mental lightbulb flashed on: the slow current drained toward the liquor store and out by some exit he had no interest in exploring at this time. That was the best he could do for a flush toilet today. He waded to where the centre court met the hallway, impressed by the increased strength of the flow of water as it entered the narrower channel. With a fleeting apology to the various shop owners along the mall, Albert made his own strong contribution to the flood.

Much relieved, he took the shortcut back underneath the stairs, triggering another greeting from Booth Girl.

Then, in the dying light and the racket of the still-noisy storm, Albert asked himself his own One Question he had overlooked all afternoon in this dead zone: *How come the booth has sound and lights?*

Albert had assumed motion-sensing devices were at work, operating Booth Girl's opening line, internal instructions and the recording. But what was powering it all? Certainly not electricity. One, the power was off all over the world, and two, if it wasn't, he'd have been fried by now. For sure not solar power, now that the earth was flying away from the sun.

Albert knew a thing or three about how things worked. He had been a technical writer back in the good old days, when his modest training had been sufficient to get him a job that would make a modest contribution to society without attracting attention. He helped turn back-of-envelope sketches into instructions and explanations that his superiors might slightly alter before they put their stamp on them. He knew that if something is to run, there has to be some motivating force. He marvelled at how often clients overlooked that little detail, expecting some gizmo to work in the middle of a cow pasture or down a well with no clue as to how it would be powered.

Carefully—as with all his movements now—he circled around the booth, looking for an access panel. There was one, of course, secured by four large, stainless-steel screws.

"Screwdriver, screwdriver, my kingdom for a screw-driver!"

A shopping mall after closing is one very bald place, a flooded one even more so. If Albert didn't have it with him, it wasn't going to be there.

Belt buckle! Albert quickly examined his belt to see what he was wearing. Nope. Metal parts were too bulky to fit in the screws' slots. But the large zipper-pull on his jacket was just the ticket.

Hastily, he inserted it in the groove of the first screw. It turned. He checked the three other screws, knowing that the likelihood of all four screws being loose was slim to none. Slim won out: all four moved easily this one day in creation. Albert unwound them all and lifted the panel off.

Batteries! A bank of car batteries were wired in sequence behind the wizard's curtain. The water was just up to the bottom of the booth. Not in danger yet, but no telling what may come.

Albert's synapses fired at just that moment to remind him of his watch's glowworm feature. He pressed the button and was surprised by how much light the thing gave in the dimness, enough for him to see the whole setup, including the speaker, playback and recording devices and motion sensors.

"Crude but effective," he said. "I could show them how to do it better. Wouldn't need this many heavy batteries."

Albert straightened up, steadied himself while his head came to terms with the motion, and entered the booth to sit and consider what to do next.

"Thank you," his only companion said. "Now, I will ask you a question and you will have sixty seconds to record your answer. There are no right or wrong answers. What comes right off the top of your head is what I want. When you are ready—"

"Be quiet, willya? I'm trying to think!"

Albert hit the ASK button impatiently as though it were a STOP button.

"Thank you," Jenna said. "You will have sixty seconds in which to record your response. Please speak clearly but there is no need to shout. Here is your question: What do you appreciate the most about your friends? What do you appreciate the most about your friends?"

"What?" he said. "What did you ask me?"

Even though Albert now knew that his friend Friday was an automaton—he had looked under her skirts and knew that for certain—the hair on the back of his neck rose just a little at this variation. She had more than one question on her programmed mind. Could he keep up with an artificial intelligence?

"My friends? Well, see—"

"Thank you very much for your help," she said. "Have a nice day."

"Not so fast!" Albert shouted. "I've had a rough day and I'm not thinking all that quickly, okay? Not a nice day at all. A very rough day, thanks for asking. Geez!"

Albert MacLean's chin crumpled then, and tears came to his eyes. Yes, indeed, Albert had had a very rough day and that day seemed far from over. How much could one man take, especially when that man was trapped in Noah's Ark all by himself with nobody but a smartass tape recorder to talk to? Plus, of everything that was falling today from Heaven, nothing was edible.

"And no pills to give me the *cojones* I need to deal with all this shit!" he sniffed.

Albert wasn't just whining for the sake of whining. He was afraid, truly afraid. He hadn't been off the pills in a very long while. While he wore his full metal jacket, he didn't care. That was the difference. He cared now and that made him afraid and that made him cry.

The yellow dome light went out. He hit the ASK button and nobody spoke.

"Ah, what now?" he cried. "Take that away from me too, willya?"

This last question was directed not at the booth but at the cosmic Whoever pulling the strings that made Albert dance to tunes he neither knew or liked.

He had to do something to take charge, to whatever extent charge could be taken given the situation.

He stepped out of the booth to check the batteries; they were still dry in the light of his treasured watch. He sloshed back to the curtained doorway and was greeted in the usual way. He stepped inside the booth and the light came on as before and young Jenna's message was the same.

There must be some kind of timer on the thing, Albert deduced, to prevent some malingerer from taking a rest in the booth and repeatedly hitting the ASK button. A malingerer like him. Clever, but alarming to Albert in his present state. Annoying, too, if he wanted the light to stay on. Also annoying to hear the same spiel over and over, Albert thought. It must be what someone with old-timer's disease is like.

"So, what do you want to know?" Albert said to Jenna, sniffing. "What about my friends, now?"

"Thank you," the student said. "You will have sixty seconds in which to record your response. Please speak clearly but there is no need to shout. Here is your question: What is your main fault? What is your main fault?"

"My main fault...is..." Albert looked directly into the sad eyes of the man in the reflection. "Just one, Jenna? I have so many. I guess if I had to pick just one, I'd say...I'd say I'm a coward, Jenna. There are more but that's a big one. If I had stood up to—"

"Thank you very much for your help. Have a nice day."

"No, wait! I want to tell you why I said that. Dammit!"

Albert hit ASK but nothing happened, and then the light faded out.

"Goddammit, what do I have to do to get some cooperation around here?" In the dark, his voice echoed in the empty mall.

Wait. The empty mall was empty also of roaring and shrieking. The windows were empty of drumming rain. Can a storm have two eyes, or was it truly over?

Over would be something, but not everything. The storm may have abated, but he was a long way from being rescued, he knew that. The water was still flooding and flowing and if this little corner of the world was any indication, many people would be in much worse shape than he, for a very long time. His modest apartment was up on the hillside and likely dry and nothing he could do if it wasn't. Might as well stick with the task at hand.

He stepped away from the booth, counted to ten and went back in, covering the repeated greetings with a loud "Yeah, yeah, whatever." He hit ASK and was ready to continue about his cowardice, but Jenna had moved on.

"What is your idea of happiness? What is your idea of happiness?"

"Oh. My. God. You see me here and now and you ask me that. Boy, do you have a lot to learn, young lady. But you're young, you've got time. What do you think would make a coward happy? A backbone, that's what. A goddamn straight backbone, one that doesn't hurt so bad that it turns you into a drug addict and a great big loser."

Jenna's voice seemed less chirpy, more soothing this time when she bade him have a nice day. It was her job, she was only doing her job, and she had to keep a professional demeanour.

In the next cycle, she asked, "What is your idea of misery?"

Albert said, "First, I apologize for my outburst there. If I sound like the cowardly lion from *The Wizard of Oz*—well, it's a long story and maybe you'd like to hear it sometime, but none of that is your fault and I have no excuse to yell at you, you're just a student doing your best, so—"

She said, "Thank you very much for your help. Have a nice day" and all seemed forgiven.

"You too, Jenna," Albert said.

There was a crash that seemed to come from the service corridor, followed by a heavy rush of water, and Albert knew the roof had fallen in somewhere. Good God Almighty, how much water would be coming into the centre court now? And would it drain out?

The batteries, the batteries, the batteries. No way he could move the booth. No higher ground to take it to anyway.

Albert closed his eyes to think, ignoring the banging pain in his head as much as he could. He thought about the setup behind the panel. He could see the wiring in his mind's eye; he knew he knew about such things. A plan, a plan, he needed a plan.

The dome light, he discovered, was converted from a flashlight and it wasn't hard to pull it out of its socket and a length of wires along with it. Albert put the apparatus into his deepest jacket pocket, zipped it up, and zipped his jacket up. No need to be careless at a time like this.

Then he went round to the access panel again and shone his watch on the batteries, water now covering the bottom inch of them. Careful to touch only one post at a time, Albert wiggled the cable connections until he found a battery with both connections loose enough to carefully pull them off.

"Okay, easy part's done," he said to his imaginary audience. "Now, this man, who has a very bad back and artillery firing in his head, this brave man will lift this very heavy very precious battery out of there and—in the pitch dark—he will carry it through swirling, cascading, treacherous waters to the stairs over there. Everybody ready?"

And that is what Albert did, with all the care and nose-between-toes proper posture he could muster. His back hummed an old, familiar tune but it didn't break out into the usual boisterous chorus.

"Now," Albert said in a low stage whisper, "we will see this genius man do something no mortal has ever done since Creation."

He unzipped the treasures in his pocket, touched the two wires from the booth light on the battery terminals, and the bulb glowed.

"And there was light!" he roared, and immediately pressed his hands to his temples.

+++

Albert and Jenna talked through the night by the light of the now-removed dome light and battery. Albert would hook up the light to illuminate the stairs, then descend and wade to the booth to hear Jenna's next question, still powered by the remaining batteries, then return to his comfy bench to give his answer at length in the cosy glow.

"What is your idea of happiness?" she asked.

Albert was smitten, in a chaste way. Jenna was but a child, maybe not twenty, and he was a man of an uncertain age. But oh, how he loved her for her interest in his thoughts and feelings, and oh, how freed he felt as he shared his rusty responses.

"Happiness?" Albert said. "My idea of happiness was a pocketful of little pills, until today. Today, Jenna, I'm learning about those pills and the misery I thought they protected me from. All they're doing is insulating me from any chance of happiness. Sure, I've had troubles, lots of people have, but I ducked and ran for cover from any feelings, any at all. And, Jenna, happiness is a feeling too, isn't it? Yes, it is, and I guess you have to risk feeling pain to get to the good parts. Anyway, all that crap that went down in my past, the job, getting hurt, getting fired, getting divorced, the one good thing the pills did for me was wrap me in a cocoon so I wouldn't feel any worse at the time. I'm still glad of that. I hope you understand. I admit I went overboard with codeine, but that's over now and that stuff is in the past and I'm going on to new things as soon as I get out of here."

On his way down the staircase to consult with Jenna again, Albert paused and said to the silent mall, "I know it won't be easy. Those pills are easy to take, hard to shake."

"What is your idea of misery?" Jenna asked brightly.

"Boy, I'm going to have to think about that one," Albert said. "Misery, eh? Hmmm." He actually smiled in spite of his pains. "You know, this morning—whatever morning it was when I came into this godforsaken place—I would've said that my whole life was misery. Now I don't know. There are people who are really, really miserable. Poor people who can't afford to eat or feed their kids, that's misery. People who get abused and can't get away, that's misery. People who get their heads in the wrong place, like I did, that's misery. But I'm not going back there, Jenna, d'you hear? Not going back."

Albert sat silent for a while and then said again, "Not going back." And he heard his sore body tell him he'd change his mind.

Jenna's next question made Albert's jaw drop.

"If not yourself, who would you be? If not yourself, who would you be?"

"Are you serious, Jenna? Who thought up these questions? How many times have I wished I wasn't me—the spineless, gutless excuse for a man that I am, I mean, that I *was*, maybe? Ha!"

Albert slumped a bit, because it was easier on his back. "I always wanted to be like my father, strong and in charge. This was his watch, see? Sure came in handy today."

Albert flashed the green luminous glow toward the booth, to show Jenna.

"He had a spine. He would never have lost his job because of an unstable filing cabinet. He would've never lost his marriage because of an unstable wife. I'd like to be my father, Jenna. That's who I'd like to be."

A few moments later Albert said, "No, I wouldn't. Maybe there's a better way to be me. That's who I'd be. Me, but better."

After a thoughtful pause, Albert said "Thank you very much for your help," in gentle imitation of Jenna's patter. "Have a nice day."

Albert sat in the booth, feet up, for the next question: "What is your favourite colour?"

"Oh, easing up on me, are you?" he laughed. "Well, I for one do appreciate it. This is a very tough questionnaire. It's been a while since I was in college, you know, and the old noggin is a bit rusty, and sore, but we're doing okay, I think, don't you? My favourite colour? Why do you ask that, I wonder? How does that fit on your charts? If I say black you'll say 'Oh, he's a very disturbed man" and if I say yellow you'll say 'He's a fruit' and if I say red you'll say 'He's angry', right? Am I right? Oh, who knows? Maybe today the colours mean different things from my day. I know I didn't like the colour of the light here in the mall in the storm. Daytime should look like day and night should look like night, and they should not fool around. It's unsettling."

He sat quietly for a while, finding it hard to remember life before all this happened.

"I do like green. It's summery, you know? Green grass, green leaves, evergreen trees. We'll go with green. Final answer."

"What is your favourite virtue?"

"My goodness, Jenna, we've known each other so long that now you're repeating yourself!" Albert smiled. "What did I say the first time you asked me? Something really old-fashioned, wasn't it, like abstinence or temperance, not that I'd know what they are. No, what was it, oh I remember: chastity. That's funny. Where'd that come from, the Ten Commandments? You surprised me with the question, that's why. Okay, my favourite virtue? What are my choices? Truth, honesty, that kind of thing? How can you pick? You need all those, you can't pick just one. I dunno. Let's say respect. If you respect people, if they respect you, then the rest will follow, I guess. You hope for that anyway, don't you," he sighed. "You hope. Hope for the best."

Albert passed much of the night in this fashion, having the longest, deepest and most meaningful conversation of his entire life, if just a bit one-sided. He and Jenna looped around her abbreviated Proust questionnaire several times more and they explored deeper and better answers each time. And sometimes shared a laugh.

Jenna remained professional and respectful throughout. Each "Thank you" sounded to Albert as though Jenna had learned something from him for which she really was grateful—until she malfunctioned for reasons he didn't dare explore in the dark.

Albert remained in his loft, then, and carried on his free-range explorations with her now-memorized questions as a guide.

Albert hadn't lost his marbles. He knew Jenna wasn't real. Sure, she was a real person somewhere and he really hoped she was all right wherever she was in this terrible storm.

In this place she was just a programmed recording, but in his present situation a little make-believe was more than understandable. Necessary, even.

He chatted and talked in a torrent of words to match the flooding water rushing through the shopping mall, keeping the gloom at bay with his tiny light.

Albert dozed off eventually, exhausted, on his firm bench. When he woke, his little lamp had burned out, but the mall was bathed in a much brighter light.

The full moon, that hurricane's tidal accomplice, was shining brightly in all its unaware glory, casting sharp shadows wherever it couldn't cast light.

The storm was over. Now all that remained was the salvage work.

Camp Pictures

The old campground would have been new at some time, but it always seemed old in memories and photos. Or old-fashioned anyway, with that clapboard siding on the cabins and main lodge being the only thing separating campers from the elements. The children laid their tired heads on crude, built-in wooden bunks or brown metal cots with noisy springs after a full day of activities. A single lightbulb hanging in the middle of the cabin was switched on in the evenings and switched off when the call went out across the field to all the cabins and tents ranged around its perimeter: "Lights out!"

These rustic deprivations, it was thought, were more likely to encourage piety and preserve virtue than private bedrooms with mattresses would have done. Rustic was cheap and easy to build with volunteer labour, too.

In latter days, the structures left rustic behind on their way to dilapidated. Fresh paint covered a multitude of sins for years, even when paint found little of substance to stick to. Still, nobody could ignore the beauty of the campground site itself. Where there's water to reflect the sunrise, where the last rays of the sun shine through soughing pines on a gently sloping hill, there's inspiration.

There were no sins there, anyway. This was a church camp, and the children who went there for their week of summer inspiration were instructed with a light touch on how and why to avoid sins, without much emphasis on what those sins actually might be.

There wasn't time! My goodness, the activities kept them going from dawn till long after dusk. The crafts, the singing, the skits, the cleaning of cabins, the communal meals. Gosh, it was so much fun. So many deep friendships were made that could last a lifetime, as many of them promised they would in the autograph books they made in Crafts Hour. Those claims—beliefs, really—were behind the tears at campfire on the last night, the long hugs as they all dispersed the next day.

Few friendships did last a lifetime, though. A week at camp was *deep and wide, deep and wide*, as the words to a favourite song went, but what lasted was more likely to be fondness for the place itself, where new perspectives or accomplishments had been awakened in the minds or hearts or bodies of children away from their homes for a whole week, some for the very first time. A wave of brotherly—if not Godly—love lifted them to an emotional mountaintop from Sunday supper 'til Saturday lunch, after which the families came to fetch them back home.

Home was a strange, now-unfamiliar world, at least for a day. Once they were home, the weight of their young lives in the other fifty-one weeks of the year soon pulled them in more directions, erasing many new lessons and loves almost as soon as they had been encountered.

Church camp was a thing of the times, the times in this particular case being the sixties or seventies. Adults who had grown up in the age of outhouses didn't mind sending their kids off to camps with outhouses that reeked of natural odours and disinfectants. Chipped enamel wash basins at an outside cold-water tap were good enough for personal cleanliness. The kids took turns washing dishes after every meal in one deep sink of hot, soapy water, rinsed them in a second deep sink of hot water with more disinfectant, and wiped them with towels that had dried on the clothesline between meals, or on the rafters over-head if the weather was damp, which some years was all week.

Camp counsellors—older teens or adults who volun-teered to look after the kids for a week—were recruited from the supporting churches' congregations. Their faith was assumed; why else would they volunteer to lead, teach, and supervise as many as a hundred children of as-sorted ages in whatever weather conditions the summer dished out? Any skills they offered, teaching crafts, singing, swimming, or outdoor games, were a bonus.

Times changed. Authorities updated public health and sanitation rules to be far less casual. Police checks be-came mandatory for adults working with children. The sponsoring church congregations shrank in size and re-sources, while costs of labour and materials grew. A week of un-focused "church" camp lagged in the race with sci-ence camp, music camp, sports camp, swimming camp, just-about-anything-else camp.

Many of these new, project-specific camps took place on university campuses, as day-camps for the younger campers, or in-residence for the lucky older ones. They awarded Certificates of Participation at the end, implying some kind of value, whereas church camp participants couldn't claim they had learned any skill that would give them a boost in life, other than how to sing a silly song with silly hand signals, which they might learn decades later had racist undertones. All the competing camps—schools, really—had flush toilets and hot showers and vending machines, and none offered old cabins or musty tents.

Many church camps ceased to operate rather than try to keep up.

That was the story of Chance Cove Camp.

+++

Long-ago campers were therefore surprised to receive an envelope from Chance Cove Camp. The envelope addressed some recipients by the name they had at camp—when would that have been, thirty years ago? Forty? More? Many of the girls had changed their surnames since those days, some more than once, and some back again to maiden names. Many of the boys didn't go by "Buckie" or "Jimmie" or "Spike" now, either. It must have taken some dedicated digging to find their current addresses at all. Some of the envelopes had at least one forwarding address written on its face, some had more.

Chance Cove Camp? What could they possibly want? Of course, they'd want money. That's what *An Invitation* on the envelope means in any unsolicited mailing these days—an invitation to donate. But still, almost every recipient hesitated to toss the unopened envelope in the recycle bin, because it was from Chance Cove Camp and addressed to them personally. It felt a little like receiving *An Invitation* from Santa Claus in the middle of summer, addressed to Little Bobbie or Little Bobby—fake, but still, intriguing. It wouldn't hurt to open it.

Besides, this was not just a slim business envelope. It was large enough to hold a magazine, and it did feel like there was one inside. Might as well have a look and then toss it.

The first thing people saw when they pulled the contents out of the envelope was a full-colour picture. The magazine's covers displayed no words, just two large photographs: Chance Cove Camp beach at sunrise on the front, and a Chance Cove Camp campfire under the pines at sunset on the back.

Almost everyone who saw those photographs paused whatever they had been doing as they felt themselves pulled right into the scenes. Those who had spent only one six-day week in their lives in those hallowed places were amazed at how they knew right away where they were.

And where they still are, evidently, judging by this package. This was no touched-up reproduction of a decades-old film photo. These were as crisp as modern digital photography and enhancements could make them. One could practically see dew drops on each blade of grass, sparks rising from the campfire into the starry sky. Someone spent good money processing those photographs.

Given the glossy introduction, the recipients wondered again, what must this invitation be about? Half still assumed that it was about handing over money. Half thought it might be about going back to Chance Cove Camp, crazy as that might seem. As it turned out, both halves were right.

Most opened the magazine. When they did, glossy prints of those two cover photographs fell out. No matter if they read another word—or any word, since none had been presented to them yet except *An Invitation* on the envelope—they would have those appealing mementos to keep.

A collage of black-and-white camp photos flowed over the inside covers, white borders on a black background, like the photo albums of another century. These were authentic originals, you could tell. The size of them and their Kodak borders were clues, and the subject matter was proof. Kids in the sixties and seventies just didn't look like kids today. Shorts and t-shirts might still be the words for what they wore, but they wore them somehow differently. They wore their hair differently, too, and their shoes, and their faces. Their expressions seemed more innocent back then, many thought, as they held the magazine up close and squinted to see if they were in any of the pictures.

And so to the first page of the magazine. It was a letter, and it began with large print that assured the reader, *Yes, you can return once more.* Beautifully-written copy followed about the dewy mornings, the starry nights, the camaraderie, the swimming, the campfires...

We know what you're thinking, the clever letter said.

> *Who wants to go backward? You've worked hard to go forward all your life, and you have achieved so much since camp days. Think of that, and take a moment to congratulate yourself. You've been learning and earning, making a home for your family and making the world a better place. Life wasn't always easy for you, and may not be easy yet.*
>
> *Some things that were mysteries to you at camp are not mysteries now, for better or for worse. But think of this a moment: where would you be now if you had not watched the sun come up over the beach, if you had not sung "The Quartermaster's Store" until you raised the roof in the dining hall, if*

you had not learned how to sweep your cabin for inspection? These moments showed you that fun, responsibility, and mystery could bring you joy.

We know they did then, and we know those moments have been with you ever since, as you met the challenges that life brought you in the decades since Camp.

Bring them alive again. With the earnings and wisdom of adulthood, you can revisit the visions that started you on your path.

This was a risky way to start a pitch, if this is what it was. Not risky if you're just pitching to strangers out of the blue, if you're just making up stories, but this was not out of the blue. It was from Chance Cove Camp, or if not actually from the church camp organization, for sure it had something to do with that place.

And that place had history. For some kids who attended camp, it was a history of just plain fun, and sweet freedom from parental supervision. For others, it was a week of misery, homesick for parental supervision. Or of bullying by other kids. Or of avoiding that creepy counsellor. Or of hating the food: enamel trays full of limp, cold, buttered white toast passed down one side and up the other of long tables at breakfast might not be expected to leave a lifelong revulsion at the sight of limp toast, but for some it had.

Also, it was a church camp, so Bible Study sessions were a stressor for some, especially those who hadn't really spent any time or attention in Sunday School and were not conversant with Bible stories. For them, the hilarious rainy-day games of Bible Baseball were sheer humiliation, as they "struck out" on the simplest of questions. Who knew if Noah was the first man, or what the

Apostle Paul's original name was, or what the heck Ezekiel saw? Scorn can be heaped on young heads for the most unexpected and unfair of reasons.

The authors of this magazine in the envelope must have anticipated that recipients who hadn't kept fond memories of dear old Chance Cove Camp, who weren't happy campers, would have tossed the complete contents at this point. Unhappy campers didn't seem to be the target market.

There was a target market, of course. The next page, and the pages that followed, laid out the product and who should invest in it. It required an abiding, or revived, interest in Chance Cove Camp, and access to some amount of money. This magazine appeared to be a prospectus, as a definition was clearly stated in the margin:

> *Prospectus: a printed document that advertises or describes a school, commercial enterprise, forthcoming book, etc., in order to attract or inform clients, members, buyers, or investors.*

The language on the next several pages was far more formal than the memory-tugging letter, describing the offering in legal and financial terms. However, more old photos appeared in the wide margins, enough of them that many hoped they'd recognize a face, or thought they did. Some saw themselves in the pictures and wondered who it was, maybe that special friend. These pictures were small, details were elusive. Someone had the originals, though. It would be fun to get copies.

The back page was a continuation of the front-page letter. *So, what does all this mean for you?* it asked, to the relief of campers who had not grown up with an understanding of investment portfolios. The answer to the question contained more but different kinds of numbers:

> *We estimate that some thirteen thousand campers attended Chance Cove Camp over the decades. Many of you would have returned several times, of course, so perhaps the actual number of attendees was one quarter of that. The records we could locate were incomplete, so we have found only about twenty-five percent of those campers' names. We expect that about one in four of those may be in a financial position to give the prospectus serious consideration, and of those, only a quarter live within a one-day trip of Chance Cove Camp.*

Having narrowed down the eligibility, the letter sharpened the point just like an alder stick for roasting weenies. There were only two or three pre-screened, pre-qualified, potential partner-investors for each of the two dozen elite sites in Chance Cove Estates. While being part of a group of fifty or a hundred children was fun 'way back when', those fortunate enough to qualify in this offering would want to visit their luxury RV at Chance Cove Estates often and spend maximum quality time there, away from the crowd: hence the small target.

By this time, keen readers were wondering how they could learn more about this very curious offer. Just below the sign-off, *See you soon*, there was a website address. Nothing more.

That seemed odd, somehow, a modern website. The photos had been a magic carpet ride back to a time when websites were unimagined, when computers took up several air-conditioned industrial rooms, when the moon was still made of green cheese. It was a time when camp kids learned to weave folded strips of newspaper into a square which they painted and left to dry in the sun, their own personal "sit-upon", used in a vain attempt to protect their shorts from grass stains. They could choose colours and any decoration they wished, so, for some, making this humble thing was the first time they had attempted to portray their personalities outside themselves. They took the precious remnants of these projects home after camp, but they quickly lost meaning and the sit-upons were discarded.

Campers didn't dream of websites back then, but here was one now. The former campers quickly logged on to the website.

It was as classy as the magazine, with the same saturated photographs fading in and out behind the words *I will return once more*. There were only two tabs on the menu bar: *Gallery* and *Join Us*.

Everyone went to the gallery first, of course, and their reward was an array of photographs, arranged by year except for one block entitled *You Tell Us*. All of them presented challenges, as the interested former campers tried to pin down what year or years they had actually been there. They looked at all the photos eventually, because some of the counsellors had gone for many years and should appear in several photos. Some campers were confused to see their faces in a group photo dated long before they remembered attending, but then remembered: their older brother or sister had gone there first. They hadn't realized how much they looked alike in that place.

The other tab, *Join Us*, revealed an invitation to attend a Reception and Information Session, to be held at an unnamed restaurant in Dartmouth in one month, on a

Sunday afternoon. The specific time would be given to those who responded.

> *This offer will not be repeated. RSVP no later than one week prior to the event by filling in the form below, using the name we have on file for you as seen on your envelope. Then send. We will confirm your reservation. No salesmen will call.*

If copies of the magazine had not already flown into re-cycle bins, many did so now. Chance Cove Camp campers hadn't grown up to be suckers for this kind of line. The loose glossy photographs, though, those were kept aside, some pinned on cork boards or taped on fridges. They were very nice to look at.

The grownup world, so far away from camp days, was all about saturated photographs, though watching a Polaroid becoming real right before your eyes had been high entertainment. Most websites and all social media based their whole existence on volumes of truly amazing pictures. But pixels on a smartphone screen could not stir the heart the way these old photos did, because the heart always belongs to the first children of adults—themselves.

It's a rare person who does not return to a recycle bin to fish out something that is, on further consideration, of interest or value. Several copies of this magazine were re-trieved after a day or night of wondering. The bins be-longing to two recipients had already been placed curb-side and the contents had irretrievably gone to the muni-cipal recycling depot. The hasty decision to cast aside that unexpected connection to childhood joined all the other hasty or rash decisions that gather in small drifts of regret in mental corners. It was rationalized eventually, as they all must be.

Those who sent their expressions of interest via the website gave it no more thought. They did make a mark of some sort on the calendar on the wall or in their device before giving it no more thought. They may have wondered where the reception was going to be, but quickly moved on to their usual quotidian concerns. A few were suspicious that this was a time-share offer; they'd heard that time-shares had an unsavoury reputation, but they also seemed to be affordable, so they gave it no more thought. Some attempted to study the prospectus pages to figure out what was being offered and how much it would cost, but they failed. That's what salespeople were for, and there would surely be salespeople at the presentation. They gave it no more thought.

Weeks passed. Those who were not thinking about Chance Cove Camp were becoming just a little annoyed at this lack of response. It seemed that Chance Cove Camp, or Chance Cove Estates, was giving them no thought either. Well, they had a busy life, and they needed to plan ahead. The lack of acknowledgement was disrespectful.

Maybe their response on the website had not gone through. Some went to it again and attempted to re-send their RSVP, but when they entered their name, the boxes turned grey and a message appeared: *Already Registered*. Well, that was something.

Another envelope finally arrived by mail for those who had indeed registered. It was a business-size envelope this time, and contained a single-page letter. The letter, addressed to the respondents by name "and guest", congratulated the former Chance Cove campers *for taking this significant step in reconnecting with who you truly are, who you have been all along.* It explained that the location of the reception was being kept private for now, to relieve those who had not registered from the temptation to drop in at the last minute. The location information would be on the two tickets that would arrive by courier the day prior to the event.

It seemed high-handed, a lot of smoke and mirrors for a simple invitation to buy a piece of land, or to buy shares in a piece of land. A bit of overreach. Theatrical. Why not just invite the public to attend a PowerPoint presentation at a hotel, set out some crackers and cheese and glasses of boxed wine, hope for a good turnout, position your salespeople around the room and play the usual games?

Also, was it too much to ask for the simple courtesy of a name, somewhere? Many went back to the prospectus again to search for a name, a person behind all this, but no name could be found. Some went online to search the company name, Chance Cove Estates, but nothing showed up.

Those letter recipients who were failing at not giving this opportunity another thought, were not married when they had been young campers at Chance Cove, far away from home for the first time. Since then, as grownups, some had married, some several times. Some had been divorced, or widowed, or both. Some had never married, were maybe single, or "in a relationship", or "partnered".

Many recipients had been reluctant to engage in conversation with their partners about this mysterious Chance Cove Camp. As the date of the event approached and the annoying game-playing went on, they were even less eager to discuss it. They knew so little to discuss. But still, if the ticket did arrive—two tickets—they'd want their significant other to come along, especially if they needed to agree to invest or borrow a tidy sum of money.

They struggled with how to broach the topic, but in the end they simply asked the spouse / partner / friend to "just have a look", to "come along for the ride". Whether by accident or design, none of the original mailings had been addressed to a couple, which is to say, not to two Chance Cove Camp campers at one address. So the invitees had to do their best to explain what these brilliant photographs meant to them and why they were now determined to cancel whatever conflicting plans might stand in the way of their attendance at the yet-to-be-named restaurant.

Responses from the spouses / partners / friends ranged from full and immediate support to mild interest to scoffing and scorn.

Invitees who were sole caregivers for children or parents or had other obligations attempted to arrange for someone else to take over for them that day, promising they wouldn't stay long. They just wanted to go to see who else was there, to see if they recognized anyone from so long ago. It was really that important, yes.

This invitation reached farther back than any school reunion had, that was for certain. This hadn't been school, anyway, it was *camp*. Sure, some kids would have gone camping in a campground with their parents, and that may have been fun, but this was Chance Cove Camp, and the parents hadn't been there. Camping with parents involved a lot of travel time in the back seat of the family sedan, with siblings or dogs and without air conditioning. How had that seemed like fun? Chance Cove Camp was six glorious nights and mornings and noons of one discovery after another, without family, without the exhausting road-time and car-sickness.

They sang so much at camp. They sang songs all the time, silly songs in the dining hall, but they were choirs of angels at Vespers, inhaling bug spray and campfire smoke, and exhaling harmonies they didn't know they knew. When it was their turn to light the campfire, they knelt and recited enchanted words—*and on the ascending flame inspire a little prayer that shall upbear the incense of your thankfulness for this sweet grace of warmth and light.* They stood in wonder at how beautiful a fresh sunrise was—the same sunrise they'd never thought to get out of bed to see at home —and recited again: *Look to this light, for it is life, the very light of life.* Sacred words. When had they ceased whispering them? Had they been replaced with better ones, or none at all?

Those who had gotten this far in their thoughts knew the answer was none: no better words had ever come into their lives. They closed their eyes and tried to bring back more of the words. *Kneel always when you light a fire, kneel reverently, and thankful be...* Amazing to find that it was still in there, wherever "in there" is where those things are stored, memory, mind, or heart. What was it they said in the morning, those who got up really early and followed the beloved leader down to the beach? *All the verities and realities of our existence—the bliss of growth, the glory of action...*

More than a few studied those photographs carefully and often. In the decades since they had been campers there, and the decades since the camp had closed permanently, they wouldn't be surprised if the small beach had been entirely obscured with bushes or debris. They would expect the old fire pit to have crumbled long ago due to frost or vandals, or the log benches around it to have rotted to nothing.

But there it was, all as before: clean, sandy beach, benches around the fire pit. Both the fire pit and the benches were new, that was obvious, and well-built. The benches in the photo were not the original old logs on the ground, either, but real benches, some with backs, built at a comfortable height for adults. And the swim platform floating just off the beach was sturdy and new.

Somebody who knew and loved Chance Cove Camp had done this work, preparing it to share with others who loved it. That came through clearly from the colour photographs. It wasn't about the money, or even about the campsite itself. It was the shared territory of childhood memory, of coming of age, of leaving home, and all those other thin, deep roots that rarely put up shoots or leaves or flowers in adulthood, but could.

What would it be like, to be in the company of people who knew those feelings at Chance Cove Estates? Of course, nobody'd be looking for those vats of macaroni and cheese ladled out at a communal table—surely that old dining hall had collapsed and been hauled away long ago. But a few like-minded families could gather together around the fire pit, and someone might bring a ukulele and song-sheets, and someone else could find that alder grove and cut some green sticks to roast marshmallows. It would be lovely to bring the children—of any age—to give them the grounding in this hallowed place that their parents had enjoyed.

What did that magazine say about luxury recreational vehicles? The word "trailer" didn't begin to describe the high-ceilinged, multi-roomed towables that were on the roads now. Most had built-in televisions, and antennas to bring in the signal. One assumed there would be internet access at the campground development now; no developer who hoped to sell any land would fail to provide that. There must be water and electrical hookups, too, and sewage disposal—standard campground infrastructure.

No outhouses. Nobody would miss those, but it would have been fun to read the names written on those old walls.

Sure, television and internet were notorious distractions in the modern era, but there was an upside. You could take in the latest entertainments or keep in touch with the office while simultaneously spending quality time in nature. If there weren't big lights everywhere—surely not—the Milky Way would still be up there.

The developers behind this yet-to-be-understood opportunity couldn't have foreseen the reaction of an unfortunate few former campers, otherwise they surely would have excluded them from the mailing. Unfortunately, their magazines arrived like landmines, and gutted the recipients without warning. Something traumatic had happened to them during their week or weeks at this humble paradise, something they had buried deep, deep inside, with no stake or pile of stones to mark its grave.

Many kids were changed in some way at camp, that was expected or hoped for. If the campers spent more time alone in their rooms at home following that great experience, it was assumed that they were missing camp, or their friends, or praying to Jesus. And perhaps some were; but some were also processing something else, something secret.

The powerful photographs spoke to the children inside the adults who received them. To a very few, they spoke in the way that pulling the pin out of a grenade speaks: with maximum damage. That deep, deep burial had bypassed memory and had settled somewhere along the central nervous system. When it was triggered, it blew, but it was not understood. Even though those photographs were selected to evoke buried experiences, the developer had surely not intended harm to anyone, couldn't have known they might.

Not all grains of sand produce perfect pearls.

Even happy experiences turned to loss for some children, post-camp. In the family sedan on the long drive home, the campers' heads had been full of songs and sights and experiences. They'd start to sing a song to their family, then realize it was a round, and nobody else in the car knew the words or the melody, so it sounded stupid. They'd proudly tell how their cabin had finally won the Cleanest Cabin award once they got everyone doing teamwork on it, and their mothers said they hoped they had learned a useful skill, then. They wanted to tell about swimming with their heads under the water for the first time, or about what it was like to swim in the rain, but they lost context. They felt like they were trying to tell stories against the wind, so they let these brave, wonderful, exciting achievements drift away. It was just too hard to tell the stories right.

They felt they had grown up in these moments, a little or a lot, back then. But they were soon faced with the hardest part of growing up: not being able to share their hearts. Everyone linking arms and rocking side-to-side gave a glimpse of a way of being that was uplifting when it happened, and oddly devastating when remembered, as they learned that it belonged only to the weightless world of Chance Cove Camp, and could not survive re-entry and the knee-buckling test of gravity.

Some didn't remember attending Chance Cove Camp at all, at first. They'd been very young, their lives ever since had many joys or sorrows, so one singular week early in a lifetime of weeks had not secured a place in their memory. But camp did happen, and the ragged memories resurfaced eventually.

Perhaps the soundtrack on the website jogged memory. It was so subtle that many didn't pay attention to it the first time they logged on. But they logged on several times, and the sound played each time, just once. *Bum ba-da bum-bum-bum*, a rising minor fifth. It was familiar, somehow. They hummed it, but when anyone asked what they were humming, many hadn't noticed that they were, and didn't have an answer.

Some did, though. Some recognized it right away, and joyously broke out into a song they hadn't sung for forty years but knew in an instant:

Land of the silver birch, home of the beaver, hum-um-um bum-bum bum, da-da da-dum.

Nobody ever knew all the words. That didn't matter. They knew the ending:

> *Blue lake and rocky shore, I will return once more.*
> *Boom-diddy-boo-oom,*
> *boom-diddy-boo-oom,*
> *boom-diddy-boo-oo-oom.*

The behavioural psychologists who must have designed this whole campaign had put the words right in the mouths of the long-ago campers: *I will return once more.* They might as well have reached right out through the computer screen and said "We see you. Sign here."

The days passed and the invitees' impatience grew. What was this cat-and-mouse game? They reminded their guest about the date several times. Those who had not yet been able to get the time free were campaigning aggressively now.

Then the tickets finally arrived by courier. Some of the recipients had been prepared for some kind of ha-ha joke's on you, send your donation here. Others still hoped hard that the invitation was real. It was.

They now had two tickets to the nicest restaurant on the eastern side of the Harbour, on the date previously advertised, in the middle of the afternoon. There was a note: the former camper, to whom the original invitation had been sent, must bring photo identification; she or he would vouch for the Guest. Guests would not be admitted without the original invitee.

Most wondered at the wisdom of this whole campaign, making it so difficult to invest in something that many people would give their right arm for, if only they knew. Oh well, they had played along so far, and soon they'd have the details.

While they waited the remaining days, more than a few contacted their banks or investment advisors to ask what borrowing power they had. Of course it was for a good reason. No, they didn't know yet what the value of the project was, or what the terms were, but they knew it was darn good, and they were confident they were being offered something that would immediately grow in value. A few were very unsatisfied with what their financial in-stitutions offered them, insulted at how skeptical they seemed to be, and a couple immediately made appoint-ments with new lenders which welcomed them and praised their sagacity.

If the original envelope had seemed like an invitation from Santa, many of the recipients now felt like the date of the reception was Christmas. They were eager, and anxious, and irritable. They had spent weeks revisiting that one tiny week of childhood, and had marvelled at how the path from there to here was so untraceable, yet it was there, for good or evil.

Who else would be there at the reception; or at the campground, should they decide to invest? Would any of the kids from their specific week or year or years be there? If so, would they recognize each other? Would it matter?

What mattered was whether or not the others valued the site, that holy ground, as they discovered they did themselves. They just wanted to be able to go back there, with their families or solo, and bask in the special sunlight, walk beneath the whispering trees, recapture the wonder of the night sky, get back something of the simplicity that had slipped away somewhere around puberty.

Nobody thought a luxury RV would interfere with simplicity. It could enhance it, as there wouldn't be worries about ticks or snakes or whatever else lived in the sod. They had heaters, and showers. Perhaps there were canoes to use, or they could buy one. There might be yoga. Most hoped there wouldn't be church, or any attempt at religion. They could have fun singing the old songs but if anyone tried to bring up religion now they'd be risking a punch in the nose.

The reception was booked at a pretty swanky place. Some checked online to look over their menu: it was pricey, appetizers going for more than a Family Pack at most fast food joints. Well, they weren't paying—or wouldn't eat if they were expected to pay, or wouldn't stay—but a few appetizers should be offered free as it was a reception, and that would be nice.

Most of the men decided to wear a button-front shirt, and the women chose something they hoped they looked good in. This event was about money; it was good to look like they had some, but not too much. They could wear shorts and flip-flops once they got to Chance Cove Estates. That was one of the nice things about a simpler life: you could shower and do your hair or shave, but you didn't have to.

They hoped the other investors there at the other sites would be kindred spirits. They did assume that the big central field—on which they had played baseball, volleyball, kick-the-ball, or whatever other running around they did—would be a common area, and that the RV sites would be arranged around the perimeter, backing onto the forest. They hoped the RVs would be spaced well apart. How many sites were they planning? How big had that field been? It had seemed expansive, but their little legs were much shorter then.

But it would be very nice if they found a friendly couple or companion who had also invested in Chance Cove Estates, who loved the old place and would enjoy sharing a coffee in the morning or a couple beers in the evening. These would be different people from the usual crowd at home who were neighbours or former workmates, a feeble basis for friendship.

A few supposed there would be a governing committee of some sort, at which they, as owner-investors, would have a say about what went on at Chance Cove, or about who was permitted to move in later. It was inevitable that original investors would eventually run out of money or die, and you wouldn't want just anyone permitted to barge in with new ideas if they didn't have roots in the old campground. There wouldn't have to be a lot of business at the meetings. Some had spent their careers in corporations or teaching and could certainly offer their expertise.

Those who had been punched in the gut when their Chance Cove Camp envelope had arrived were torn about going to the reception. If they had registered in time, they had received tickets. Would they use them; and if so, why? Why open old wounds? Would the ghost that haunted their dreams for so many years be there? It was unlikely that they would invest, but maybe someone there would like to hear their story anyway, the so-called allegations. Or maybe they wouldn't bring it up at the reception, but if their experiences were ever brought to light, it would be good to have some contacts from this swanky presentation. They might eventually find somebody to accuse, to make amends, to sue, or to send to jail, or whatever they did with people like that. If they told.

There were a few invitees who had not forgotten one remarkable second of their time at Chance Cove Camp. They might have put their fond memories aside out of necessity, but they had never been far away. Why would they be? Their time at camp had been the pinnacle of their lives in many ways. They had freedom there, without their uneasy, overbearing parents telling them to stop, hush, share, pray. At camp, they watched the family drive out the lane, and then they were *on*.

They laughed, they teased, they wielded the tea-towels drying on the line like whips, which stung like them. They sang loudly and out of tune, they argued with the ump—adult or child. They splashed, they knocked perfectly roasted marshmallows into the pine needles. They brought musical instruments they couldn't play, and they played them after lights-out. They weren't the bullies, but they sure were needy.

The counsellors were not skilled in dealing with these outliers, kids who were too noisy or too quiet. A private talking-to was considered punishment at Chance Cove Camp. Early dismissal almost never happened. Those noisy campers would certainly go to this reception.

Maybe they'd dig out that old straw hat with the dingle-balls all around the brim, and arrive ready to pump up the sound again.

If there was a memory or emotion that that fancy magazine, the intriguing website, or the glossy photographs hadn't yet evoked, it would surely erupt at the reception, stimulated by the memories of others. The representatives of Chance Cove Estates had better be prepared to deal with the adults who now embodied the children evoked by their prospectus.

When the day and time finally arrived, all those ticket-holders who could invest, or wished they could invest, or were certain they would never invest, made their way to the restaurant. As they walked toward the entrance, each felt disoriented, as if they were going to a familiar place which they'd never seen before.

They hoped they would find something good there, something they needed.

+++

Inside the restaurant, Chance Cove Estates representatives waited and watched, relieved that years of preparation were finally going to play out and pay off.

They had envisioned and brainstormed this, multiple times. They market-tested and focus-grouped it. They consulted behavioural psychologists, sociologists, cultural anthropologists, and fiction-writers. They engaged the marketing firm with the best creative team. They found the best improv actors and created the characters they would play. They workshopped scenes like they were developing a Broadway musical.

The players had visited Chance Cove several times to explore every natural feature of the place, including that big submerged rock that little kids could swim out to and stand up on, the trail that led away from the field and looped back, and the sound of the breeze in the tall trees. They hired a landscaping company to prepare the site, and an award-winning photographer who waited patiently for the rising and setting sun to appear just so.

They had mined social media and business groups to extract a vast amount of information about the former campers whose names they were lucky enough to find. They obtained credit information about as many as possible, and adjusted their initial and long-term financial arrangements to match what the best buyers would find easiest to bear.

They had quietly observed the homes of today's registered guests—from the outside, of course, nothing creepy or illegal here. They took pictures of them coming and going, and memorized their faces. They learned if there were spouses or partners, and what kind. They engaged lawyers to advise on every statement they wrote and every step they took.

They expected the afternoon would conclude with more investors wanting to sign up than there were sites available. It was first-come, first-served. Sites could not be placed on hold, as other buyers would be standing in line, ready to commit today. Keeners might miss out if they hesitated—or if a representative discovered they didn't fit the corporation's strict eligibility profiles. They would be distracted with busy-work until it was too late to buy. The presenters had prepared for the unknowns, too.

But they would offer the indecisive and the disqualified other options, other interesting properties to invest in where they wouldn't be sharing time and space with people they didn't fit in with. Everyone would go home with something they valued, believing that their friendly advisor had just given them a great deal.

Chance Cove Estates had methodically invested time and money on preparation, and were confident of success. They knew what would take place in each of the ninety minutes that were about to unfold in real time. They were as prepared and confident as their prospective clients were not. And they were incentivized.

"Oh, good. I see my client has arrived," said one representative. "Let's do this!"

"Mine too," said another. "He looks exactly like I thought he would. We're going to get along very well."

"Places, please, everyone," their leader stage-whispered from behind the bar. "Showtime!"

About the stories

I was alone on a long south-to-north road trip. I find that the car is the perfect lab for generating writing ideas, and I was hoping to find some twist in familiar texts to use in a story. It doesn't have to make sense to you, but for the next eleven hours I recited nursery rhymes as prompts.

> Mary, Mary, quite contrary, how does your garden grow?

No inspiration there.

> Twinkle, Twinkle, little star, How I wonder what you are.

Better. I love the tune, but found nothing to exploit in the lyrics.

> Little Bo Peep has lost her sheep, and doesn't know where to find them.

Interesting. Christians have been talking about lost sheep for millennia.

> Leave them alone, and they will come home,

That's not what the Bible says. It says to leave the ninety-nine sheep alone, and go rescue the one that is lost.

Wagging their tails behind them.

A bit of nonsense there, but—as you read in *The Church of Little Bo Peep*—the Good Book has nonsense in it too if you've a mind to look for it. The literary possibilities sprouting from this centuries-old rhyme entertained me on the long route home, and eventually became the foundation of this wandering tale.

I'm not the first to mine alternate meanings from Bo Peep. My story mentions a comedian in the early 1950s who achieved fame doing just that. You can see his performance here:

https://youtu.be/hdaeQLCTa6g

I think comedy has changed for the better since then.

Side story: my Grade Eight teacher used to quote snippets of Standley's routine in class. I didn't find him funny either.

While wintering in Florida, I heard that a "church of prosperity" was opening in an industrial park nearby. Curious, I attended a service—just one—to sample the vibe. It was an impressive operation, and pure carnival. I'm familiar with scripture, but I'd never heard the words twisted as they were there. I found it deeply disturbing. I incorporated that mega-church into my Bo Peep story, but not as humour.

Homelessness isn't funny either, but it does provide an obvious turning point for a smart fellow determined to rise up.

I was sitting in a coffee shop in a large mall, which is what I do when I say I'm going shopping. In the concourse just outside the café were several kiosks. The one nearest me was selling makeup, and a slender young woman presided over the display. She constantly scanned the crowds, letting dozens of women pass by without approaching them. When she chose a mark, she would walk beside her for a few steps, long enough to say, "Excuse me, may I ask you a personal question?"

Rarely did her chosen customers fail to stop. She followed that question with a compliment—I could lip-read the thank-yous—and a suggestion that they might like to try a jar of whatever she was selling, a daub of which she was already rubbing on the back of their hands. She sold many jars while I sipped my latté.

Later, when I went out into the mall, she didn't offer to ask me a personal question, but I didn't expect her to. She sold only to women who wore makeup.

Her question stayed with me, though. It wasn't "Can I show you?" or "Would you like to try?" It was intimate and polite and charming. How seldom are we offered questions that invite us to explore and share our feelings, and not just yes or no?

Near that kiosk was one of those brown photo booths, tucked next to a stairway. I don't know if it was working, but it seemed anachronistic next to the make-up vendor and her magic potions. There was also the ubiquitous array of child-size rideable snails and turtles that rocked or rolled when coins were inserted. I didn't check to see how many coins it would take to start them up. Maybe my spending the equivalent of a car payment for coffee wasn't really out of proportion to the cost of other temptations in the modern shopping arena.

In *Ten Questions*, mall fixtures and the questions they pose make one very weird day better for one man. This story loosely employs the Proust Questionnaire, a parlour game from the late 1800s[1]. Forms and variations are still used, frequently on CBC Radio 1's "The Next Chapter"[2]. These random questions can reveal characteristics about people that perhaps they hadn't known about themselves. The questions may be more respectful than just saying, "Tell us a little bit about yourself," which implies that there is only a little bit to be told.

There is a degrees-of-separation kind of link between *Ten Questions* and *The Church of Little Bo Peep*. Arthur isn't aware of it, but you may be. It's fun to read about a fictional character in a story and say, "Hey, I know who that is!"

+++

I attended summer church camps as a teen, and led summer choir camps as a young adult. I had many of the positive experiences related in *Camp Pictures*, and none of the negative ones—unless you think of well-used outhouses or cold flabby toast as negatives. I didn't.

I tried to imagine the many emotions those glossy photos from Chance Cove Camp would or could evoke. Would former campers remember the experience as a time, or a place, if they thought of it at all? How would their memories begin to resurface? By asking the standard list of questions, of course—who, what, where, when, and why. Also, in this instance, how much.

---

1 wikipedia.org/wiki/Proust_Questionnaire
2 cbc.ca/radio/thenextchapter

People on both 'sides' of this story's proposition used the same questions, unaware or deliberately. The same questions, but different: "What will I do?" vs "What will she do?" Even so, everyone's pretty sure they have answers.

Ah, answers. Let's leave them for another book, shall we?

Jan Fancy Hull

I am deeply grateful to Moose House Publications for publishing these stories, and especially to editor Andrew Wetmore for making my writing better, with kindness and grace.

Jan Fancy Hull

About the author

Jan Fancy Hull lives in a log chalet beside a quiet lake in Lunenburg County, Nova Scotia, where she has written poetry, fiction, and her debut non-fiction book, *Where's Home?*

Prior to arriving at this idyllic position, she served in various careers, enterprises, pursuits, and avocations, including, but not limited to, arts administrator, radio broadcaster, sailing tours skipper, and employee benefits broker.

In the warm months, Jan creates sculptures from Nova Scotian sandstone, which she exhibits in various galleries and shows. She is currently active in the Lunenburg Art Society. She also enjoys golfing and drifting around the lake in a tiny rowboat, but doesn't do enough of either. There are so many things to do.

Website: janfancyhull.ca
Facebook: Jan Fancy Hull

Sneak peek: *January: Code*

Here are the first two chapters of *January: Code*, the first book in Jan Fancy Hull's **Tim Brown** mysteries.

January: Code will be available for December, 2021.

Subscribe to our website, moosehousepress.com, to get news about this and other Moose House books.

January 6: The call

"Happy 1999, my dear aunt!"

Tim Brown always skipped "Hello" for this caller and didn't wait for her to announce herself. She insisted that having caller ID dispensed with the need.

"We already went through that on the day, Timothy."

"Yes, we certainly did. Happy Old Christmas then? Or Epiphany? Does one say Happy Epiphany? If I had an epiphany I'd be happy—"

"I didn't call to chatter, Timothy," Stella said. "I have something for you to do."

Chastisement or chores were the usual reasons for calls from Stella, though Tim was nearly forty and Stella was of indeterminate age. They were the only surviving members of the prominent Johnson family of South River. Tim cared for his aunt, but he often paid for his affection. She knew every thread, apron string, and nerve connecting him to her, and she had no qualms about plucking any or all of them if she had something to gain by it.

"I'm listening. Do tell."

"I need a driver. When can you start?"

"Me? Um, let's see. Never? What are you talking about? You want me to be your chauffeur?"

"Yes. Mine has—I have dismissed the one I had and I require another one, especially in the winter. You aren't working, so I'm offering you the position."

"You mean you want me to help you find yet another driver. How many's this, now?"

"Focus, Timothy," Stella said. "I am offering *you* the work. It requires no skill other than keeping my vehicle safely on the road and ready for me whenever I need to come to the city, or go to South River or other locales. And discretion. The remuneration is superior, of course."

"Sounds peachy, Aunt Stella. But it's not on my career path, thanks anyway. Besides, I am *not* looking for a job. I am now on my long-desired and much-deserved sabbatical."

"And why have you abdicated your position at *The Times*? It was perfect for you. You're too young to retire. Your mother and grandfather didn't labour as hard as they did so that you could coast while the paper ran itself into the ground, so—"

"Don't forget great-grandfather, too," Tim said. "But hold on, now. I did *not* abdicate, I haven't retired, and I am *not* coasting—"

"But you're not at work. You've told people that you're going to be a sleuth or some such thing. Shouldn't you know something about that pursuit first? Study law or police work, at least? Apply for a permit? Not that I would recommend it as a suitable line of work for someone in our family."

"Aunt Stella, I have told you and told you. I *am* going to work, just not as Editor and Publisher of *The Times*, not for this year. I'm taking a sabbatical, which surely is my due after devoting every moment of my life since I was in junior high school—"

"Your mother and I and our antecedents did the same —"

"And where did that get you and our antecedents? Grandfather had a heart attack. Grandmother went insane. You ran away from home and joined the convent. Mother died in the saddle. I think taking a sabbatical is the only way I will survive to go forward, and if all goes well, I'll return to the paper invigorated and ready to—"

"Doing what?"

"Beg pardon?"

"What will you be doing during this so-called sabbatical, then? I had no inkling that you aspired to become a gumshoe."

"A gumshoe—oh dear and merciful God. That is so *film noir*. You're a drama queen, Aunt Stella."

"What I am is very concerned to see you wasting the inheritance that we have placed in your care."

"Aunt Stella, please listen up and listen good, as long as we're talking 'gumshoe'. Here's what I said I would do and what I *will* do. I said I want to delve behind the news, as it pleases me to do, to examine the usual issues that concern a community newspaper like ours, and try to find a different perspective in general and maybe something interesting in particular. That's what 'delve' means, to examine a subject in detail. At *The Times*, all we do is take a picture and slap some words under it and there it is on the front page of the paper: Rising Tide Floats Boat. Then we're on to the next thing. You know what that feels like? It feels like—"

"I know what it feels like. I was close enough for long enough."

"Then you understand the attraction of delving deeper."

"Not in this context, I don't. You'll be trying to do deep spadework in a shallow cookie sheet, Timothy. There is no 'deeper' in this small town or, by extension, in its newspaper. Your main function is to support the town merchants and organizations by carrying their advertisements amidst bits of screed pretending to be journalism."

"You think my editorials were just filler, Aunt Stella?"

"Let's not get sidetracked."

"Yes, let's not. But if I *was* writing screed, that just strengthens my argument for a sabbatical. But there *is* no argument. Our new interim editor is doing fine, so I'm off for at least a year. I will not be 'sleuthing.' I will not be sitting in my sparsely-furnished office with a pint of whisky in one pocket and a pistol in the other, waiting for some gorgeous dame to hire me and nearly get me killed by her jealous boyfriend."

"Fat chance."

"Thanks. How I will do my delving I cannot say exactly because I don't know yet. Preconceptions are the enemy of discovery, don't you agree?"

"Oh, you're a philosopher now, too, are you?"

Tim sighed loudly, deliberately blowing into the telephone mouthpiece. "As usual, Aunt Stella, you chase me into a corner. I don't need to defend my decision nor will I argue with you. With regard to your—um—job offer, I decline with thanks. But I'll keep my ear to the ground for you. I may run across someone who fits the qualifications, you never know."

January 7: Choir practice

Stella phoned again.

"If you insist on investigating, I have something I want you to investigate, and it may well be dangerous. Now listen: something big is being planned or is going on in South River. It may be very important, may have serious implications."

"Really? I can't wait to hear what that will be. Ever since the old mall closed, there's—"

"I know you were born and raised and educated to some extent in South River, which is not your fault, but a strip mall closing or opening here would hardly have serious implications. Or be secret."

"I suppose you're right," Tim said, "though these days simply a new pharmacy generates attention. So what is it, Aunt Stella? A secret, you say? I promise to forget as soon as you tell me, then."

"I don't *know*, Timothy. I'm asking you to find out and tell me. I know—from impeccable sources—that *something* is going on. As the Member of the Legislative Assembly for South River and The Harbours, I'm the one who should know about and announce major developments. Or denounce them, if that is what's called for. Not some other so-called personality, or a federal politician who is not as in touch with the electorate as I am."

"Well, I'm stumped. I'm not aware of anything 'major'. Perhaps you'd better ask the Premier. Why not call my interim editor at *The Times*? We report on every business that advertises with us, you know."

"I am privy to some high-level conversations and I also, shall we say, acquire intelligence by other means. In the hands of someone less attuned to goings-on, this information would be just assorted bits of noise. However, I believe I have indications of something very important to the region, maybe critical. I need you to find out what it is."

"You want me to tell you what your jig-saw puzzle picture is without even seeing the few pieces that you have?"

"Exactly."

"No clues?"

"None at this time."

"Is it an old mill scene? A basket full of puppies? A mountain stream?"

"I could not answer you even if your questions made sense. But make no mistake: it is something very important. Pursuing it could be dangerous. I urge you to pay close attention to what I say, as I don't need you getting yourself shot. Do *not* be tempted to play the gumshoe. When you learn something, bring it to me and I will sort out the wheat from the chaff for you. Am I clear on this point?"

"Aunt Stella, you are sounding exactly like the movie dame I was describing. I could get shot? I somehow find that an unattractive job offer. We'll see, okay? That's the best I can do for now. Tonight is choir practice and Robert does *not* like to be late, so I will say ta-ta for now. We'll talk of this again, I have no doubt. How about dinner next Sunday? It'll be just we three for the usual exquisite loaves and fishes. RSVP by next Wednesday, please."

"Us three," Stella said. "If meetings do not intervene. I will advise."

The call ended and Tim noticed a slight moistness on his forehead. Talking with his aunt on the phone often felt like a physical workout, and she was an Olympic wrestler when she wanted to be. But she was also an occasional and welcome dinner-guest. She enjoyed visiting for an evening at her family home with her only living relative. She obeyed the rule that controversial topics must be avoided during dinner at risk of not being invited back. She craved the delicious menus concocted by Robert, and she coveted any selections from Tim's wine cellar.

Robert was waiting in the foyer, jingling the car keys. "What did the Duchess of Muchness want this time?" he said, smiling. "I couldn't help overhearing."

"Nothing I could figure out," Tim replied. "She just wanted to talk. She sends her love."

+

Choir practice was every Thursday evening in the choir loft of Saint John's United Church. Saint John's had no particular historical or architectural significance except that it was huge. It had been built in the thirties by Tim's great-grandfather a few years after the denomination was founded. He had assumed that a uniting church would eventually swallow all similar faiths, so he—and his agreeable peers—built it to accommodate the whole population of the growing town.

South River's population did grow, but so did its collection of sects, factions, and denominations, while Saint John's became the town's centre of cultural activity. It was an acoustically excellent space, could seat a thousand people, and eventually possessed a splendid pipe organ, so it attracted performances that most towns of triple that size couldn't think of hosting.

The construction and ongoing upkeep was funded generously and almost exclusively by Tim's great-grandfather's endowments. Even as the congregation dwindled through the century to a fraction of what he had envisioned, there was no shortage of funds for overhead or salaries at Saint John's. Preachers, assistant preachers, and lay staff, including the director of music and other specialists, were recruited and handsomely paid.

Situated just over an hour outside Halifax, South River was a reasonable commute for city talent, making it possible for Robert Kirk to take on the position of Director of Music at Saint John's after the previous incumbent had finally surrendered the organ bench. Robert was an accomplished church musician, taught organ, harpsichord and music history at a university in Halifax, conducted the university's two choirs, and carried on a respectable performance career as organ soloist. He didn't need to add Saint John's to his roster of duties, but he was attracted to it when he met Timothy while on a concert tour, and the opportunity to play the church's famous organ had sealed the deal. He stipulated a refit of the instrument as a condition of his appointment, which was completed for a minor fortune without a peep from the church trustees.

To play that organ was why Robert was eager to get to the church this evening. He intended a new postlude for Sunday and he didn't want to sight-read the piece on Sunday morning. Not with his students in the congregation for an elective credit.

While Robert worked at the organ console in the sanctuary, choir members arrived in the adjoining church hall in singles and groups, with much stamping of feet and hooting about the cold as they entered. It was early January, very cold outside with frozen dirty snow on the ground.

Twenty adult singers can make a lot of commotion. A sticking door that clanged when it was opened from the inside in response to thumps on it from the outside, coat hangers clattering on metal rods, and greetings exchanged by people who were there because they were sopranos, altos, tenors, or basses, all contributed to a happy racket. Robert preferred not to hear it, so the choir was excluded from the loft inside the church until summoned.

The buzzer sounded in the church hall to signal that Robert was ready for the choir to enter. Those who shared stories of slipping on ice, worries due to threats of layoffs at a nearby plant, joys of recent Christmas family reunions, or sadness caused by long winter days all took their places in the lineup. When they emerged into the loft they had melded into a Choir.

This Sunday's sermon was to be entitled "Paying for the greatest gift of all on credit: how God's people deal with Christmas bills." The senior minister often strained to be relevant, and several choir members greeted this particular reach with soft groans. Not only were they sure they wouldn't enjoy the sermon, they would be seated only three meters behind him while he delivered it. They would have to appear attentive, or at least impassive, and certainly not amused, since they faced the congregation.

"Okay, people," Robert said. "Manners! Now, for our anthem, since we've nothing special prepared due to the Christmas blow-out, I have advised the Reverend Doctor that we will sing *Nun Danket* by Mendelssohn.

"No, it's not in your folders," he said as choir members began to search with concern for this new piece. "It's hymn number 333, 'Now Thank We All Our God'. Seems appropriate enough, considering the sermon topic.

Second verse in unison, please, while I attempt a *faux bourdon* to gussy it up."

While Robert played the hymn's introduction, Tim's fellow tenor, Spencer, leaned close to Tim's ear and said, "What's that? Half a devil?" His finger was pointing to the 333 in Tim's hymnal. Spencer was no comedian, but he was a constant joker.

Tim gave his eyes a half-roll as they stood up to sing:

> *Now thank we all our God, with hearts and hands and voices,*
> *Who wondrous things hath done, In whom His world rejoices;*
> *Who, from our mothers' arms, Hath blessed us on our way*
> *With countless gifts of love, and still is ours today...*
> *And keep us in His grace, and guide us when perplexed,*
> *And free us from all ills, In this world and the next.*

Tim's conversation with his Aunt Stella popped into his thoughts as he sang those final lines. Talk about perplexity. What *ills* had she been referring to? Why had she called him to investigate her big mystery? Why not one of her minions at the Legislature or her legion of party supporters? What should he do about her request? He knew from experience that he must comply or lose an arm and some of his dignity in refusing.

What did he intend to do with his 'sabbatical', anyway? Into what was he going to delve, exactly?

Nagging at Tim was his own fear: the behind-the-news subjects he had been looking forward to delving into offered only deeper dullness, shallow mines of valueless ore, like gravel pits or cookie sheets, as his aunt had suggested. Tim had been focused on his transition from the newspaper for most of the past year, ensuring that a competent person was contracted to take over his responsibilities of editor and publisher. Now that was done, Tim saw that the end of his all-consuming new line wasn't tied to anything: he was adrift. His compass needle was spinning, not pointing.

At least he needn't worry about income. His small-town, family-owned, only-one-for-miles-around weekly had generated excess income from its inception, and would continue to do so as long as spending didn't exceed revenue, as his late mother had often reminded him. The business owners who couldn't keep their greedy fingers out of the cookie-jar, she said, would fail this simple primary test.

Tim remained perplexed for the duration of choir practice, through the good-byes following, and for the rest of his evening.

+

Intrigued?
Subscribe to moosehousepress.com
to be among the first to know when
January: Code is available.

www.ingramcontent.com/pod-product-compliance
Lightning Source LLC
Chambersburg PA
CBHW070500200726
48293CB00007B/2310